# Dancing
# in the
# Asylum

Fred Johnston is a writer, journalist and musician from Galway, Ireland. He has received the presitgious Hennessy Literary Award for prose, the Sunday Independent Short Story and Poem of the Month awards, and more recently the Prix de l'Ambassade. He co-founded The Irish Writers' Co-operative, and has published four novels, eight collections of poetry and had three plays performed. He has lived in Algeria and Canada, and spent a year as a writer-in-Residence to the Princess Grace Irish Library at Monaco in 2004. This is his first short story collection.

# Dancing in the Asylum

Fred Johnston

PARTHIAN

Parthian
The Old Surgery
Napier Street
Cardigan
SA43 1ED
www.parthianbooks.com

First published in 2011
© Fred Johnston
All Rights Reserved

ISBN 978-1-906998-44-8

The publisher acknowledges the financial support
of the Welsh Books Council.

Editing, cover design & typesetting by Lucy Llewellyn
Cover photograph: Nancy Honey, Millennium Images, UK
Printed and bound by Gwasg Gomer, Llandysul, Wales

*'L'homme doit vivre seul. Aimer, c'est abdiquer. Haïr, c'est s'affirmer. Je suis, je vis.'*

Herve Bazin: *Vipère au poing*
(pbl Bernard Grasset, 1948)

*for Mary*

# Contents

# Dancing
# in the Asylum

'He could only think clearly in the dark...'
Sean Dunne: *Wittgenstein in Ireland*

Pritchard didn't know where he was.

Then it all came back to him.

There was a prickly white haze around him; the bed was too white, insubstantial, though he could feel himself lying on it, under blazing white sheets. The room was white – he could not judge its length, breadth or height – and the figure at the end of the bed was draped in a raging white gown.

The figure bent in two and Pritchard felt something very sharp stab the sole of his right foot.

'Feel that?'

Pritchard grunted, trying to unsquint his eyes and at the same time to defuse, reduce, the glare.

'That?'

His left foot this time. He grunted again. With each sting something of memory tried to insert itself, push through. His head was swathed, not unpleasantly, in thick coils of grey, dull fog. So long as he could not remember, he was safe. But the prodding of unspecific, oddly menacing thoughts, went on.

Another figure in white stood at the foot of his bed and, reaching down, withdrew something. A long, brown, wooden plank. Pritchard felt the plank shift under him.

'You won't be needing this.'

The voice was devoid of the least inflection of emotion, as if its owner were stoking a fire or replacing a flat tyre. Pritchard's eyes, the lids sticky and hot, were opening, taking more in. The room was not white after all, but painted a utilitarian mix of green and cream. It was long and had other beds, some of them occupied. Floor-to-ceiling windows – barred – were all around him. It was a well lit, boring room. The ceiling was very high, a pale clouded sky of plaster. Noises came to Pritchard, distant shouts and a laugh and a tinny clatter of something. There were footsteps.

The male nurse and the doctor straightened up at the foot of his bed. The doctor smiled vaguely, a prematurely bald young man in glasses. The male nurse was spotted with facial acne and had red hair. The doctor glanced at Pritchard's bed-foot chart and grimaced, then smiled again.

'You had a skinful, Mr Pritchard.'

Pritchard tried to sit himself up in the bed. Under

his neck and head, a pillow moved awkwardly; he reached behind him to try to fix it. His hands were sweating. As the sheets moved, he took in great gulps of a pungent, metallic smell. Alcohol sweat.

'Take it easy, now, Mr Pritchard. Just relax, sleep whenever you can.'

When Pritchard went on benders, sleep dissolved. So did eating. You couldn't sleep, didn't want to anyway, with the sort of dreams that sleep dragged in. Besides, sleep wore away the effects of the drink; and then, well, Pritchard knew what happened then. In the numbing, hallucinating, mouth-gummed, gasping, terrified, muscle-jerking, wanking-to-calm-the-nerves early mornings, in the tangy roaring dawn.

No, sleep was no friend. Worse was to eat. After the first few days, eating anything made your heart beat uncomfortably, maybe even dangerously, you could feel it through your shirt; you sweated, the shakes came in too early, too fast, and, what was worse, the food filled a space in your belly which could not be taken up with more drink, so you had to gibber through a sobering-up you'd induced yourself and it was terrible. You walked and walked, trying to slow down the banging heart, feeling the legs give, twitch, jelly in the gut, everyday objects growing terrible, and everyday sounds menacing and threatening. All the time you were angry and defiant and muttering threats to yourself and against yourself as you walked and thumped your frail

3

thighs with balled fists, hating and hurting, hating and hurting. And you were appallingly tired.

Eating and sleeping were out, definitely, when Pritchard went on his benders.

'A nurse'll be around shortly, Mr Pritchard. Do you know where you are?'

Pritchard felt a sudden rip of anxiety cross his chest. The foggy coils around his head began to slip. No! If he said he was anxious, maybe they'd give him something.

He sat up, the iron, flaking bars of his bed-head touching cold against the back of his neck. He was remembering, it was all seeping back.

'Yes, I think so,' Pritchard said. His voice was not his own voice, it was someone else's.

'Do you recall how you got here?'

The young doctor's tone was hoarse with authority. Anyone, thought Pritchard sadly, can have authority when I'm in this state. Fuck him.

'I'm not a hundred per cent sure, doctor.'

Pritchard was irritated by the quiver that hobbled his voice. The frailty, the tearfulness. Be a bloody man!

The young doctor seemed satisfied. He enjoys this, Pritchard thought. He enjoys dealing with people on the edge of the horrors. He can't deal with real people, people who could speak back to him, tell him what's what, the prying, over-privileged little fuck.

The doctor and the acne victim dislodged

themselves from Pritchard's aching vision. The male nurse swung the wooden board under his arm, like a rifle. They moved – insolently, Pritchard thought – to another bed. In this one Pritchard saw, when he turned to look, a very old man – with a drip attached to one Belsenesque arm – who was snoring loudly. The doctor inspected the man's chart, raised his eyebrows, made a note, walked on.

It came back to him, drip-fed. He'd allowed himself to be talked into doing something about himself by that idiot, ten years younger than him, a pup to interfere, Andrews, who just happened, of all the luck, to be in that pub. Andrews, whom he'd worked with, once, shared the same office.

Andrews had his job. Andrews licked arse, that was how. Andrews, who had the cringing impertinence to suggest Pritchard had a drink problem. Only problem is where to get it, ha-ha! Andrews, the office bend-over. The lackey. Always correct, always this and that. Had Pritchard's job now. Pritchard had no job at all. He was on the dole. A poisonous monotony, the indignity, not right for a man who's been through university, all very fine for the underclass uneducated and the like. They make money on the black, in any case. Watch porn-vids all day. Do the horses. Talk with every second word being fuck. Know nothing of the greater picture, politics, the world. Never read books. Lining up with the likes of that on a dole queue, you need a drink. Everyone does, besides. Poverty does that. Not having money. And the wife. The arguments. Makes a big thing out of breaking a plate; the thing never touched her, I threw it accurately where I threw it.

Laura.

Pritchard remembered he had a wife. And a child, a five-year-old called Danny. Their faces came, wearing pleading looks, out of a now-parting fog and with these images came more heart-scouring anxiety, a drawing of a Brillo pad across the red, meaty, surface of his plodding pump. They arrived as faces from a past he was not sure he had ever inhabited. Suitcases left unclaimed on a deserted railway platform. They brought fear. Had he murdered them? Even now, were police driving to this place? Led there by Andrews?

He hadn't murdered them. His heart slowed. He just hadn't seen them for a while. A week. No. More. Best part of a month. Where he had spent that month was another thing.

Pritchard clasped his hands around his mountaining knees. The old man's snoring had subsided; cars drew up outside, somewhere below and to his right. A cacophony of coloured noise spread along a corridor, which, he noticed, ran parallel to his bed. There was a world out there gathering itself; the hospital, if that's what this place was, like a lumbering ship, readying itself to set sail into another day.

But not every hospital had iron bars on the windows.

6

He'd precipitated some incident. That was always the beginning. Part of him knew he had started it, always did.

Another, stronger part, declared once again that Laura was a pain and had niggled at him about something; yes, he hadn't taken the TV down to be repaired, or bothered to call somebody, it hadn't worked for ages. She'd raised her voice.

He hadn't hit her, not that time. When Pritchard thought of the times he'd struck his wife he felt a coarse-grained mixture of repulsion and fear. She had brothers. He wouldn't have had to strike her at all if she'd just shut up. But Laura seemed to invite him to do it. Well, no relationship was perfect. In the pub, everyone said that women wanted only to dominate men, get the claws in, and they had to be told.

He'd slammed the door behind him. Laura slobbering away, Danny screaming. Danny was always screaming and it was clear to Pritchard that Laura and he were raising a wimp who'd be bullied at school and probably for the rest of his life. I was an executive before I was thirty, Pritchard had told himself. Danny'll never be anything.

Pritchard loved his son. Drunk, at night, he would be overcome with emotion and he'd wake his son and tell him stories to put him to sleep. Tears would fill his eyes. I love you, son, he'd say, and kiss his son tenderly on the head. I would kill for my son, he'd declare out loud in Danny's airplane-wallpapered little room. Any father would. And when Laura would stamp in, whispering irritatingly that Danny had been nicely asleep until Pritchard had woken him, he'd have to remind her that he was the child's father – He's my son, so fuck off! – and Danny had a right to know his father loved him and would die for him.

Now that he thought of his wife and his son, however, Pritchard didn't feel pride or anger, just a limp, wet fear. They frightened him. Just the horrors, Pritchard reassured himself. You know this dance.

A nurse came round with a trolley laden with pills and pads and all sorts of things. She was young, wore a tight white uniform that showed Pritchard the outline of her white panties and gave him a nervous erection. Nurses are always game, he reminded himself. Everyone said so.

She leaned over him, plumped up his pillow. Pritchard could smell the girl's aroma, a clean, warm, maddening hint of powdered sweat and soap. Her eyes were dreadfully brown and moist. Half my age, Pritchard thought. I am growing old. She doesn't see me. She does; I am but meat on her tray.

'Now, Mr Pritchard,' the young nurse said in a sweet, musical voice, a voice from crossroads' villages, wide green fields, and the hot buxom smack of summer. 'Take these and this cup of water. Drink it all, now.'

She handed him two round cream-coloured things.

8

Rubbery texture, you could press them in, there was a liquid inside them. Duck-eggs; he'd heard of them from old-time drinkers. Pritchard drank mostly with old-timers, wrecked-looking, redundantly knowledgeable men who shook always and borrowed money from him in the early-houses, pubs opened from dawn. Sometimes he borrowed from them, hating and enduring their reluctance, their ungenerosity, their sudden dislike. Educated man like you must have money invested, they'd mock. Cackle-cackle.

In pubs that open before the sun was up, the smell of disinfectant and lavatories and stale cigarettes all over the place, everyone there frightened and shaking and trying to put a brave, stupid, macho face on it. That he had to borrow money from the likes of them made his skin crawl with delicious violence. He wanted to strangle, gouge, stab. But he took their money and drank on. The revenge was to make them ask for it back. Show them who's boss.

One day, he'd just borrowed a couple of quid from one of them when the man grew a sudden rictus on his face, staggered, and fell to the just-mopped glistening tiles of the floor and went into convulsions. No one moved to help him. The barman, boredly, reached for the telephone. Someone must have offered him a job, croaked a voice from somewhere on the bar-stools. He's an epileptic, said someone else; That's why he gets fits. He drinks too much, the barman had said.

9

But no one had wanted to hear that. Pritchard, soothed and arrogant with the man's money in his pocket, spoke up for them all, the final word. Drink never did anyone any harm! Everyone agreed, soothed. The ambulance arrived.

It was in a pub just like that that Andrews had found him. Pritchard, against his better judgement, had been trying to eat a toasted cheese sandwich. He'd been washing it down, tenderly, carefully, with whiskey and water. He had almost no money. When he saw Andrews, he smiled broadly, showing a mouthful of mashed cheese and bread, and extended his hand. He congratulated the younger man immediately on his promotion.

'You'll do a great job,' Pritchard had said.

'Thanks,' Andrews had replied, stiffening.

'Like my office?'

'Pardon?'

'Your new office used to be my office.'

'Frank,' said Andrews in a slow, priestly tone that made Pritchard very angry indeed, 'You haven't been in that office for almost two years. Davis was in it last.'

It was then that Pritchard had remembered that Laura had told him about Andrews' promotion. He wondered how his wife knew. Things tended to come back to him in a domino sort of way, one revelation knocking into another: Andrews's wife and Laura had always been close friends. Always talking about me,

10

Pritchard knew. Women together, demonising the men.

'I know,' Pritchard had countered admirably. 'But I left my mark on it, didn't I? It has me written all over it. Like slipping into a well-worn suit.'

Andrews had smiled, looked away. Victory to me, thought Pritchard. But he had not been ready for the younger man coming back at him. Not like he did.

'You look desperate, Frank,' Andrews said. His voice had a dark edge to it. Pritchard wondered whether Andrews was a closet gay. 'Laura has gone and taken Danny. Now, before you ask me, I don't know where. But she's serious this time. So Helen tells me, anyway. You know they're close.'

Going home, sobering up, the three-odd days and nights in bed sweating, shouting, pissing, retching, seeing things, hearing things, shaking, Laura his safety net, always there, cleaning up, changing his clothes, feeding him hot milk and toast. Danny watching from the bedroom door; these things had comforted Pritchard, they'd kept him going. He could drink in peace, knowing the net was there for him.

Gone, Pritchard felt the empty soundless cold void of the house swell inside him, assume his shape. The terror of it almost made him choke and his heart was starting up, accelerating.

It came back with the gloves off, now, Andrews trying not to look at him, the bearer of bad news who just wanted, job done, to get away. Something like fear, but slippier, crawlier, began to invade him, just remembering it. He'd offered Andrews a drink. There had been a vomiting sound from behind the smashed door of the Gents. Traffic clashed and bantered outside the long, pale, dirty window with the brand name of a whiskey distillers' in peeling gold leaf on the glass. A smoky, impish light filled the room.

'Well, what am I supposed to say to that?' he'd said, turning into his drink. It was whiskey and a pint of lager this morning, he wasn't feeling very strong. Andrews had not gone away. He had stood beside him. Like a beggar, Pritchard thought.

'You should stop this,' said Andrews. 'What you're doing to yourself.'

'If she's gone, she's gone,' said Pritchard. The pain, the terror, was indescribable. He gulped whiskey, gulped beer; it got worse. Andrews had seemed to fidget, a player who no longer understood his role, who'd forgotten his lines, the cues askew. Andrews spoke like a figure in a dream.

'You're a mess. Look at you. This can't go on. You know it can't.'

'Who the fuck are you to say what can and can not go on!'

'No one, you're absolutely right. I'll go.'

Broken free of his reverie, Andrews seemed to acquire strength. He turned away. Pritchard had felt him go, fall free of him. More terror, more being alone.

12

'Fuck you, don't just go!'

Andrews stood a few feet away. Heads turned at the bar, something was happening, something to look at. Pritchard felt their eyes on him.

'I've lost my wife.'

They looked at him, not caring, not knowing him. He felt their unclaimable distance, the false promise of affection he looked for every time he came in here. At the same time, horribly, he thought of his wife and his son. The pictures were always head-and-shoulders shots and always sad. They looked like refugees, at the mercy of the world. His nervous system screamed out in the language of bitter anguish and self-pity. It is not they who are alone, thought Pritchard, seeing himself as a small boy in a big room crying and nobody hearing him; it's me. I am the lonely one.

Andrews had come closer. Pritchard regarded him in those black, chilled moments with a mixture of pity and restrained, almost homicidal, rage. Under the lonely sadness, this rage, an anger that had no name, anonymous.

'My wife's left me, and my beautiful son,' Pritchard said. 'She's taken my beautiful son.'

The tears that came relieved nothing. They dribbled and were sticky and hot and salty when they reached his mouth.

Pritchard saw himself and what was happening as if were stuck to the ceiling, somewhere up in the air

13

and off to his right. He was in a grotesque movie, in a particularly poignant scene. So he knew the tears came with the scene, the part; he could not be convinced his emotions, any of them, were genuine, not part of a role he was playing. The bar was a set and everyone was in on it. Besides, he'd used tears and hysterical collapse dozens of times before to compel Laura to change her mind, even when she had her coat on and a taxi called. Life had become, more or less, a series of petty roles; occasionally the performance came off and sometimes it did not.

This time, however, Pritchard surprised himself. His chest heaved and the drink he held in his hand spilled and slapped loudly and flatly on the floor. Andrews was holding him. He was crying real tears and he couldn't stop.

'I'm fucked,' Pritchard said into Andrews' shoulder.

'More or less,' said Andrews.

Pritchard recalled now a taxi ride, a reluctant driver, the light of the city far too bright, too bitter, an argument. He went in to bright lounge bars and Andrews dogged him, watched him, even paid for some of the drinks. They were being drawn inexorably towards a conclusion, there was no avoiding it. Perhaps he had even agreed to it, it was impossible to tell. Something had broken in Pritchard, something had moved him one square nearer a chasm into which

14

he had always dreaded to tumble. Now he strolled its lip, pursued by a young man he had never wanted to know, who knew him too well for comfort.

Pritchard recalled a different taxi, a new argument, nothing; then a doctor relieving him of a small bottle of whiskey and Andrews waving goodbye, sun all around him in yellow dollops as he left through tall double doors.

A soothing halo of egg-yolk light circled everything he looked at. There was a pane of thick glass between Pritchard and the threatening cold world. He was up, now, steadying himself on pale, thin legs, wearing someone else's pyjamas, trying to hold the bottoms up with one hand. He felt weak. Every step brought a louder thudding of his bruised heart. The ward seemed to be a vast and luminous cathedral, filled with unearthly golden light, almost liquid, spilling over the polished wooden floor, the white beds, the still, quiet walls.

He stood upright and moved, one step, another, in a dream of floating and rising and falling. On a bed – it seemed so very far away – a figure in a dark suit, a suitcase at his feet. Pritchard moved towards it. The figure moved, cowering, grabbing at the suitcase. Pritchard felt his face smiling, though it felt wet and cold and not his own.

'Cigarette,' said Pritchard. He didn't know why.

'I'm going out,' said the figure, crouching, knees up, on the bed. Pritchard shrugged his shoulders, felt the fabric of the raggedy, ill-fitting top of his borrowed pyjamas drag nastily over his skin.

He turned back to his bed. He heard the soft, panicky shuffle of slippered feet behind him. Then, from a very great distance out in the corridors, he heard yelling and impatient shouts. This was followed by a heavy silence. Pritchard looked up at the gleaming, glowing bars on the fire-flecked tall windows. He felt terribly afraid and chokingly fragile.

Pritchard sat at a long table in a tiny dining room. A huge crucifix shadowed them all; the Christ-figure was twisting away from them, fed up with them. Around him, a dozen men of various ages sat like children. Orderlies brought trays. He didn't feel hungry, just very frightened and subdued. Everywhere the light was strange and striped with jerky rainbows.

'No chicken soup for him,' an orderly said, just as a very old man was about to dip his big, trembling spoon into a steaming soup-bowl.

Pritchard watched the old man's expression of utter helplessness as the chicken soup was lifted away. The world was very small now. Even chicken soup had become mysteriously dangerous, fatal, loaded with terrible possibilities. Nothing was certain, there were no borders around anything and yet everything was bordered, nothing permitted.

The soupless old man jumped up on his seat and started to scream.

The bizarre folded into the ordinary, bright, multicoloured layers of events and shards of conversations. Pritchard moved around the ward behind a dozen others, walking in a shuffle-shuffle circle like camp inmates in old, scratched newsreels. This was exercise. No one spoke. An ancient man dribbled and muttered to himself – the old man of the chicken soup episode had evaporated. Pritchard tried to strike up a nerve-jagged conversation with the man in front of him. He spoke to the back of his head, a pitted neck.

'What are you in for?'

The man grunted and bowed his head. Pritchard had been trying to be funny. There were things groping and crawling their slimey way up from his memory that he did not want emerging into the light. A joke, he'd thought. Something funny. A dirty joke, a chat about nothing. But Pritchard was whispering in the kingdom of the deaf and dumb.

Later he tried to open a door. He was right-handed, but his left hand kept shooting out, pawing the door knob ridiculously. Then he tried a game of chess, sitting on the bed, surrounded by men in pyjamas who did not speak, with someone who'd bothered to talk to him and offer him a cigarette. He ended up playing with the other man's pieces, the other man playing

17

with his, a perfect, upside-down, inside-out game, a mirror map of his new found land.

No one noticed. Pawns came and went, a Queen lost here, a Knight here. Pritchard laughed like a maniac, a laugh filled with tears, when he and his opponent, at the same instant, like tripping a switch, realised what was happening. Ha-ha-ha-ha-ha-hee-hee-hee-oooh-hooh-hooh!

The lights yellowed and a sort of ominous, rattling hush smoked down the corridors. There was nothing permanent here, no feeling that long, imaginative lives had touched the utility-painted walls or explained themselves within the vacuum of these sucking halls.

The warm air was chilling, underneath everything lay a soft murmur comprising every sound or word ever spoken in the place. Trapped in the still air, sounds lived over and over, language froze. Pritchard imagined that if he stood still and listened he would overhear scraps of conversations had by men who'd paced these halls before him. Nurses moved unregardingly from one annexe to another, swiftly, whitely, with untouchable determination.

A very ordinary door had a little red sign with the letters E.C.T. engraved on it.

Passing this door, Pritchard smelled the unmistakable tang of burning hair. His heart banged and walloped as he imagined for a terrible instant men coming for him in the night, tying him down, convulsing his terrified body with electric current. He felt helpless in this place, at the mercy of unknown and vengeful gods. There was nothing at all in this walled-in universe over which he had the slightest control.

Pritchard and his chess opponent wandered as far as they could, looked down corridors brilliant with the light of silence and sedation, inhaling always the mixed intimate incense of stale cigarettes and disinfectant. They stood under a high square of window and watched a fingernail sliver of moon balance itself in a blue-black sky. The window, twenty feet up, had its ration of iron bars. The moon settled between them, imprisoned too.

They inspected the TV room – ancient magazines, newspapers, an ancient black-and-white set – and there, standing back as if privacy mattered, Pritchard's companion pointed out to him, rigid among the formica-topped tables and the plastic roses, and men sleeping in old-fashioned tubular lounge chairs while the ash grew on their cigarettes, a grey-haired, white-faced man who, in his tartan dressing-gown, was staring at himself looking back out of the TV screen.

Music started up; the man leaned from one foot to the other and with an idle hand conducted into thin air as the precise, interesting musical notes fled out over the inert bodies in their dead chairs and the rising whisps of cigarette smoke.

On the TV, the documentary programme was now listing off the man's achievements. Pritchard heard a

19

litany, ponderously retailed, of symphonies, a quartet piece, a commemorative anthem.

The composer began to cry. A thin, reedy note came out between his tight lips as if he played his anguish like a musical instrument. Fat, silvery tears plopped on to the lino squares at his feet. All the time, various white-haired versions of himself flitted and smiled and bowed across the shaky TV screen.

He stared and cried until a nurse, small and fast in her white uniform, scuttled from nowhere. She spoke gently, soothingly and changed the TV channel. She got a documentary on Nazi Germany, all grainy, with martial music. The composer stared at this, too, crying.

Unsettled, Pritchard excused himself and made off into the lavatories armed with a vague image of the nurse's bum. Several times he had found release from nervous tension – his neck would wobble, his hands would twitch – masturbating in the brown-wood cubicles. The doors had no locks and no latches, so he'd had to keep his door shut with his foot, which made the whole operation pleasureless.

Night came. With it fell over them all a sort of exhausted composure. It was possible to read. Pritchard found a dreadful paperback somewhere – the place, he discovered, was a warren of somewheres – and found he could read it, follow the words in some sort of sequence, quite well. A shadowy, mechanical whisper, warm and enveloping, draped itself over the ward and the long, religious windows. The creamy light of the hall was comforting. He knew he could not get out. The door in the hall was operated electronically and controlled from a nurses' station in a distant reach of the corridor. He'd tried it. There was no handle.

But nothing could get in, either. There was solace in that. The world was outside and far away.

I need rest, Pritchard thought. I have laboured in the world and found it wanting.

Pritchard thought about God.

A nurse came round and gave him one of those rubbery duck things, Heminevrin capsules. He smoked and considered God. He felt cosy and warm and cared for and imagined that, in this state, he could easily believe in a benevolent and bearded face, a cloud-bound Burl Ives, smiling down at them all.

He did not know where he was but that was fine. Everything would work out. It was warm here, and dark, and people were around to look after you and lock out the pestering world. Laura and Danny were on the other side of a thick wall of smoked glass that could only reflect, reflect forever, their gaping and bewildered images, back, back, into the darkness of an uncomprehending world.

Pritchard thought about them and felt absolutely nothing and fell asleep.

Then he felt noise all around him. He opened his eyes stickily, afraid.

21

Light slanted down from the great El Greco windows, early, cautious sunlight. Figures moved in beds all over the ward, hesitating, grumbling, coughing. Pritchard had soaked his bedsheets with sweat; his heart was doing its old hard, bone-bruising tattoo. He felt for his balls, squeezed them for comfort, felt the beginnings of a dubious, timid erection. His head teemed with thoughts of all kinds, little fishes with barbed fins that scraped at the inner arches of his skull. He lay there on his back and felt his breath go, panic tightening his chest. My heart will explode, he thought. It was too early, too early.

Pritchard felt a warm needling up and down the backs of his hands. When he closed his eyes and plunged his head under the comparative grey shade of the bedclothes, an enormous single eye gaped at him from behind his own shut lids.

It was surrounded by smaller eyes, watching him.

He pulled himself out over the sheets again, gasping for air. He struggled to haul himself into a sitting position. He groped on his locker top for cigarettes; one inhalation teased his nerve-ends to the point of shredding. His bare arms looked thin, terribly white, strengthless. His mouth was dry, clotted with night-ooze from his bad teeth, and his breath stank. His sweat smelled of iron and earth. He wondered whether he would have a seizure, if he'd swallow his tongue, if he'd lesions on his brain. He felt his throat muscles constrict with tension and drive him into a hot, panicky melancholy, a sadness sudden and pointless. In the brazen light of early morning he and the others twitched raggedly in their beds, exposed once again to their cold hells.

Walking about – he couldn't face breakfast, the mug of scalding tea, the toast, the egg, but he took the pills – slowed his racing thoughts. Moving about seemed to have that effect on everyone else; everyone walked, going nowhere, back and forth, up and down, sometimes as far as a window.

The world outside was a car park, a row of flailing trees and a slap of green. Pritchard went to the window too. He looked out and saw how green everything was, how blue the sky, how white the clouds. Colours were solid, strong, brilliant. He found that his gaze fixed easily on things, held, as if every object in the world, small or large, was hypnotising him. He could calculate by now just how long it took the pills to kick in, how long before he stopped wanting to scream in fright to be let out.

A trolley came by; Pritchard ordered more cigarettes. And a newspaper. He wasn't asked for money. The orderly moved on, pushing his rattley, silver trolley. The little black wheels clicked and whined quietly over the tiles.

Pritchard stood in front of the crucifix in the empty dining room. The silence of the long bare table was harsh and cruel. The Christ looked down into his eyes from between half-shut lids. The blood on the hands and feet was too red, the thorns about the agonising head looked as heavy and blunt as stone.

Pritchard, swaddled in his own silence, felt naked and transparent, as if the painted eyes of the figure could see through him, see everything that lurked there, and yet they retained an expression of crafted indifference. What did you really look like? thought Pritchard, the question heavy with unbidden, drugged emotion. In the midst of alcohol withdrawals, Pritchard knew, men said and thought very strange things, most of which they later regretted and shrugged away. You were probably black, his thoughts went on without him. An intellectual moving among the plebs, speaking in riddles.

Pritchard was preparing to think something snide and smart about the figure on the cross. But an ancient, long-buried, schoolboyish pity rose up in him from a well of similar unlabelled pities. Against himself, against what he really wanted to say and feel, he found himself in turmoil looking at the twisted, sculpted figure. This is just my nerves, he told himself, and left the dining room. Outside in the bustling, agitated corridor, he breathed in deeply, let the lump in his throat subside a little, ashamed of himself. In my state, a sad fairy tale would have me a quivering wreck, Pritchard reassured himself. It will pass. It always has.

A pretty young nurse came over to him. Her approach terrified him. What were they about to do to him now?

'Mr Pritchard,' said the pretty, country nurse, smiling and showing perfect white teeth. Pritchard looked at her teeth, stared at them, but she didn't seem to mind. 'Your wife telephoned. She will be here to see you tomorrow around the beginning of Visiting Hours, about two.'

The nurse turned and walked away. Pritchard took a deep breath and burst into tears. He sat on the edge of his bed – nurses, busily, impatiently, had made it up, supplied new sheets, removed the old ones rotten with the glutinous mould of his nightsweat – and stared, wet-eyed, through a broad shaft of meringue sunlight in which dust motes swam like so many tiny sea-things. They moved in a silent, eternal ballet, up and down and sideways, choreographed on frail drafts of hidden air.

He smoked until his cigarettes ran out. He could not move. Emotions twitched in him, changing, hurting, elating, teasing, out of control. He was their prey; they nibbled at his ribs, his lungs, the lining of his stomach, the outer walls of his wobbling heart, crowded the dripping corridors of his skull. He began to sense that he was invisible. In moments of true sorrow, you became invisible. The human eye denied you.

The first time he had seen his wife had been at a

25

performance of an opera by Handel. Laura liked Baroque music. Pritchard had only gone because he received free tickets through the office.

Two colleagues accompanied him, under his cajoling, to take the bare look off things. The opera was Berenice and all Pritchard could recall about it was what the programme said, that Handel had suffered a stroke shortly after it was performed at Covent Garden in 1737 and that it hadn't been a great success anyway. Attracted by nothing in the opera's plot or music, Pritchard had been drawn quirkily to the fact of its failure and the collapse of its composer. Perhaps, he would often think in times to come, failure and breakdown had been on his mind for some time already.

Laura had been sitting one row down from him. All he had seen was the white glow of light on the side of her face, the way it seemed to emphasise her, as if her skull were lighted from within. He saw her cropped hair, as it then was, and the play of light over it, glossing it.

The girl's profiled beauty seemed enhanced by the music; the conjunction of the two caused something deliciously warm and unfamiliar to move inside him. The music began to take on new meaning, rise to new heights of interpretation, because Pritchard was looking at the girl and because he found her beautiful. Pritchard was not used to such feelings, they were not his thing.

Unmanned now, Pritchard recalled in frightening detail every event of that evening; silly, predictable, young man's events, chatting up a girl, buying her a drink, making a date, the usual. Ha-ha! So funny, life is!

He had struck her, Pritchard recalled, and Danny had witnessed it. A long time ago. It returned, now, a memory with a razor edge, slicing through the drugs, the fags, his soul. He had broken up the house, the kitchen at any rate. He had smashed the TV. He had screamed in rage and frustration at nothing at all. He had pissed himself in their bed, his bed, Laura's bed. Handel had suffered a stroke. He recovered, he recovered. He had used the open palm of his hand, wasn't that not so bad? The rise, fall, and sweep of that precious, thin music. The light on the side of her face, the rest in shadow; like a Venetian carnival mask, the yin and yang of possibility, the what is and isn't.

She was coming to see him.

Through everything – was she that bloody deranged? – she was coming to see him. Not today, tomorrow. The hours would drag and there was no way of knowing what she wanted to see him for. And would she bring Danny? Nothing to do, thought Pritchard, sniffily. He peered into the shaft of light; it looked solid enough to clamber up, escape through the plate glass, through the bars. Pritchard shivered. His chess opponent was shuffling his way towards him, moving in faded, lopsided tartan slippers over

27

the glowing, disinfected tiles.

Pritchard didn't want company. He had no strength left for anyone. He felt hungry, tired, vacuumed out. If Laura would have him back – so was Andrews shagging her or not? Where did they do it, so? Not where Danny could see, surely? – he would change. This time it just wasn't a formula of words. He needed her, the world was too large and frightening a place without someone.

He remembered, hurting at the memory, that there had been a girl somewhere over those recent lost days and nights, a girl who had laughed at him because he couldn't manage an erection. A girl he'd met in a pub – in these days of AIDS, he'd risked that? – and he couldn't recall how far they'd succeeded in going, but she'd taken him to her flat and had been gone when, shiveringly, he'd opened his eyes on the next morning. Blue panties with a pair of fingers in a V-sign over the crotch, lying on a Santa Claus bedside mat.

He'd picked her up. Perhaps it was the other way round. It didn't matter. Pritchard tried to recall what she'd looked like. He couldn't. Thinking about her at all was terrifying.

'Can I interrupt?'

The chess player stood over him. His body odour was laced with the drench of nicotine. Pritchard looked up at him, aware of his red eyes.

'Have you a fag?'

'I have indeed.'

They sat together at the edge of Pritchard's bed and smoked.

'My wife's coming tomorrow,' explained Pritchard. 'I've been pretty ugly with her over the years.'

The drugs, presumably, were making him feel confessional. He pictured himself sitting on the hospital bed with this man, smoking, talking his life away. Drugs or not, he felt a deep and impossible desire to describe himself, his life, what he imagined made him the way he was. The closeness of the man – their pyjama'd thighs touched – was not unpleasant. There was an odd calm with it. Pritchard felt better just having the man there.

'It's good she's coming,' the man said. 'Mine never did. Not after the first couple of times. Don't have a clue where she is. No children, thankfully.'

'They pulled a plank out from under my bed,' Pritchard heard himself say. The urge to explain, to reveal, was overwhelming.

'In case you had a seizure and hurt your back.'

'Where exactly are we?' asked Pritchard.

'Oh, on a good day you can see the sea from these windows. Or the mountains, looking another way. Nice views, really.'

They sat in silence again. Their cigarette smoke curled upwards, blew frantically into the shaft of sunlight, took on weird and marvellous shapes, hieroglyphs.

Pritchard felt the fidgety tug of more unpleasant memories, images forming, unforming, something from a half-remembered and very sloppy movie.

They sat on the edge of the bed and around them the musical framework – Schoenberg as opposed to Handel – of the corridors and rooms and doors and windows swelled and faded.

Pritchard considered Laura's love of music, a sense of taste which she had never been able to pass on to him, her instinct for what was good and what was vulgar. And Danny, and her wish to have him take up piano lessons. Money, Pritchard had thought; a matronly lady with a long skirt and spectacles turning the greasily-thumbed pages of ancient musical scores. Pay by the hour. Waste.

He sucked on his cigarette and stared at the tiles, their dirty cracks. He would give anything to prove himself a good father to his son, husband to his wife. But how was so much rubble restored to a former glory; how could their little citadel be rebuilt?

He would get his job back, Andrews might help there. Was Andrews screwing his Laura? Pritchard felt a spasm of sorts, a light electrical charge, run down his spine. Sitting was uncomfortable. He got up, the man left sitting on the bed watched him. He felt like walking, each thought caused a new shiver in his spine, up the back of his neck.

'A bit jumpy? Natural.'

The man's tone conveyed a sense of infinite patience with bodily discomfort, of acceptance of things that twitched and pricked. 'I can't shut off my head,' said Pritchard. He tapped the side of his head with a shaky finger. Little pulses of electricity passed into is skull.

The man grunted. Pritchard remembered the odour of burning hair. Images came upon him in a rush, hot and maimed. It had nothing to do with him yet it was about him and from inside him, it oozed out of his heart, liver, stomach, kidneys, from a smoking molten throbbing in the very pit of his brain.

His heart revved up again, valves that could do with some oil. They would come for him, strap him down, attach electrodes to the sides of his head, shoot him full of electricity, burn his nerves, his skin; they would come as he slept, or in the bright cold terror of the morning.

He had always known they'd come for him; they'd been coming for him ever since the day he'd been born, disguised always, often just out of sight; but they knew him, knew how terror fitted him, and in here they had him cornered.

He began to sweat yet again, though his palms and mouth dried up. He was panicking, his breathing tighter, each breath shorter and shorter, compressed by some increasing pressure on his chest. The walls of the room were closing in, the floor tipped at an angle. The

31

ship was listing. He wanted to hurl himself at something, throw something out of the way, escape. The panic was in his throat, closing it. He couldn't breathe; the cigarette fell from his fingers. The man stood up. Pritchard opened his mouth like a fish and nothing went in.

'Panic attack,' said the man, and crab-walked out of the room. Pritchard fell across the bed. A nurse came in, did something. He slept.

When he woke up, the lights were out. Only the calming light of the corridor broke into the warm dark. He lay for a long time staring up at an invisible ceiling, calmed by whatever the nurse had given him, resting deep in a soft cocoon of bedclothes and medication. Once again, and gratefully, he felt snug, protected, comforted. Again, there was the notion that the big bad world could not find him. He was safe. Hard as he tried to think bad, invasive thoughts, he could not. Something soft and warm and rubbery inside his head stopped the poison leaching through.

Pritchard lay there for a long time thinking of nothing.

And then the music drifted over him like thin whisps of smoke.

He was breathing the music long before he heard it. He thought it came from the ceiling, from the sky. Around him, awkward men snored or dreamed loudly or whimpered in their sleep. Someone would be awake, wide-eyed, masturbating, terrified, somewhere in the long-windowed room.

Pritchard listened to the music. It came through the walls. It was part of the building's masonry. He got out of bed.

He followed the music, its tendrils of notes and cadences, and he moved out into the corridor. In the subdued light's clinical silence, Pritchard felt vulnerable and cold. Holding his pyjama bottoms up with one hand, he moved in bare feet very slowly along the corridor, led by the music.

The nurses' station was some distance away and in shadow, but even now Pritchard could see there was no one on duty.

The music was louder. It came from beyond the door at the very end of the corridor. Pritchard got to the door and, as he had anticipated, it was locked. But Pritchard still felt safe and snug inside his portable cocoon; nothing could touch him, everything was possible. He felt free. He went to the nurses' station, leaned over the desk, found the button. He pressed it. There was a light hiss and a click. He went to the door without handles and pushed it open.

The soles of his feet froze against the icy tiles. He was somewhere else now, beyond the borders of his friendly, known ward, and mercifully alone. A sense of mischief hooked on to a rising sense of fear. If they found him here, he knew what they'd do to him. But

33

he couldn't stop himself, he couldn't go back, not now. He moved on, past doors through which snoring and the other sounds of frightened sleep could be heard, past corridors which seemed to have no end beyond darkness.

The music was loud now. A half-naked man came out of a room, stared at him, giggled, and went back in. Pritchard moved on. His feet shuffle-slapped, warming up. He felt very normal, ordinary. He had a right to be here.

He turned a corner. Through the massive wooden archway of an opened door the music crashed and bellowed and flowed like lava, hot in his ears, gushing from the building's heart.

He approached the door. Someone, the half-naked man, pushed past him, eager to get inside.

It was a sort of gymnasium, wall-bars, ropes coiled carefully up towards the girdered ceiling. Nurses moved with orderly caution around the walls. A male nurse leaned over a turntable, raised on a sort of wooden dais at one end of the room, squealed indecipherable things into a microphone, adding to the noise, flanked by black, net-fronted speakers taller than a man.

And in the middle of the polished planked floor, men were dancing.

Dancing with each other, half in and half out of pyjama trousers and tops, round and round in friendly circles, a galaxy of beats out of time with the thud-thoffa-thud of the music.

Pritchard slid down the side of the open door, sat propped against the wall. His ears became accustomed to the noise, the impish wailing of men on the floor, the shouts of the male nurse DJ. The nurses moved about the wall, dancing a sort of sarabande of their own, round and round, a few steps at a time, anticlockwise. They watched everything, but no one noticed him.

Some men broke free of their circles and clap-slapped their hands together, staring at them, marvelling that the collision of their palms gave birth to a sound.

One man twirled round and round on his own in the middle of the floor, then squatted down and removed his trousers. A nurse glided with the grace of a ballet dancer to where she could lift him up, at the same time securing his trousers, all of it like choreography, she lifting him to his feet as he raised his arms, then let them fall slowly. Another man left his circle and began pummelling his face with his hands and shouting over and over a single word Pritchard could not make out. No one came near him. He performed alone.

Pritchard felt smug, confident. He could see, now, the pattern in it all. He could see the unity of which he and these men were a part; it was a sort of cube, transparent, and lukewarm to the touch.

No one had told him there was such a place as this. Where music played and men danced, danced however they chose to; where a circle of angels moved around them, chorusing, chanting, the universe comprising layer upon layer of their humming and the dancing of other spirits in their holy circles.

This was the innermost chord sounding at the heart of a contented God. The great In Nomine. You witnessed this, you were privileged. Blessed.

Pritchard tried to think of bad things, but they couldn't get in. Nothing, no one, could penetrate here. He heard the footsteps, the march of them, the solemn warning of their tread, coming nearer and nearer down the corridor behind him.

Round and round the madmen danced, round and round the angels circled, sublimely out of step with the music yet formed by it, a component of its every note and beat.

And Pritchard felt strong hands lift him to his feet. He did not resist. He stared and stared, burning the sight of the dancers into the black, scrawly screens of his eyes.

You never got a chance like this again. These things, you saw them once, you understood them only once, and the rest was darkness.

# At the Reichstag Hotel

'The yelps are faint here on the strand.'

Seamus Heaney: *Girls Bathing, Galway 1965*

They irritated him.

There were so many of them, always laughing at nothing. As if the air were a feather-cloud of laughter, you only had to reach out and pluck laughter from nothing.

Some of the girls were beautiful. The milk chocolate of their skin, the nut-dark glister of their eyes. And their beautiful black hair. The thin boys, pocked with adolescence, their voices absurdly loud. A mad, unapologetic energy here. He had never known such energy. He had never possessed a sliver of it.

Rain came down in hard explosions on the road, on the roofs of cars, scattering the young foreigners. He envied them. The green sloped square darkened under the rain, everything turned back to its usual grey. The reds, the blues, the yellows of his world turned watery and cold.

'Stand in.'

A fat woman, grandmotherly, looked at him, beckoned with her head. He should do what he was told, stand out of the rain. The young foreign girls screamed and laughed as the thick rain matted their black hair and splashed on their thin tight slacks and jeans.

'Our Irish summer,' he said. The woman nodded. There were hairs growing from a large mole on her cheek. Her face was creased like a leather purse. She carried shopping bags. Her bulk seemed to nail her to the ground. Out of the pub behind her came a young girl struggling with a buggy. The infant tucked inside screamed up to a pitch almost beyond hearing. The girl fought and angled the buggy, tried to get it through the door but couldn't manage it. She was talking to the squalling infant as if it were an adult, chiding, trying to work it out of her system. He looked at her, felt no inclination to help her. On the contrary, he felt angry. The girl was too young to have a child. The world was out of control. How ignorant could she be?

'I'm not responsible,' he said, to no one at all.

The fat woman took a bus. He crossed the road in front of the hotel. It's granite black front, the pillaring, the arabesques and the long windows reminded him of some venerable edifice he'd seen in a book. Germany, was it? The Reichstag building? The hotel's imposing face seemed to lean slightly over him as he walked past it. They burned it, didn't they? He could not recall where he'd seen the photograph and began to wonder as he walked whether it had anything to do with Germany at all.

He read so much, books on everything and anything, his wife said; as if describing a disease. He wanted to write a book, was writing a book. He wouldn't tell her. She had no business knowing, this was private. He had told someone, but that was different.

The book was his way of forgetting his wife, the house, his life, for that matter; he knew this, could say it out loud, but he wrote carefully and deliberately nonetheless, remained diligent about his research. He was serious about his book and felt the warming comfort of that seriousness. He wanted it to be published, in the end. But he feared finishing it, he was afraid of that, normal enough.

He got into his car, grudgingly paid the parking attendant in his little wooden box, a sullen tabloid-scouring sentry in a ripped hooded Army jacket, and he drove out into the slippery roads. He judged the distance between his front bumper and the rear bumper of the vehicle in front of him, knowing nasty things could happen when the road surface had been dry and was then suddenly drenched. He drove carefully, third-gearing up the gritty hill, the traffic slow anyway because of the time of day. He turned on the radio and heard a young girl's voice describe heady events happening in a High Court room. He wondered

39

what she looked like. Her voice was delicious to him. Her voice was yesterday and the day before that. The days he had not lived.

He disliked any kind of sport, thinking it unnecessary. He turned the radio off. For a second he risked a glance at himself in the rear-view mirror. He saw the lines still under the eyes, the scrappy thin hair. He saw that his neck bulged in his shirt-collar, the way he was sitting.

The bay opened up to one side, silvery under the sudden late sunlight, and the castle watching over it blackened in its stone by the rain, and the mountains over the bay, sullen and blue under their thatch of cloud. No one lived in town anymore. It wasn't smart. You moved out, not far, just far enough, into the country. The line of vehicles, in front and behind, moved along at a slow, morbid pace, and a rat ran sloppily across the road in front of him, just making it to the wet green hedges.

He wanted to take his wife to Spain this year. Or Italy. He enjoyed writing postcards and letters from distant places. It made him feel, well, happy. It was a form of play. He liked to play. Grown men should be able to play. Just like children.

'And do you ever think of going home?'

'No. Never.'

He'd watched the boy's eyes, their shallow, dirty movement, thiefy. He'd hoped they might reach a point where they might talk. But the boy seemed seldom to be really present. Had he a home?

'You never say much about your home. Your family.'

'Fuck all to say about them. They're crap.'

Perhaps that was the best word. Crap. To describe so many unfixable things, so many monsters no one, certainly not God, could ever tame. My wife is misshapen, overweight, has let herself go to seed. She was beautiful and amusing once. Our children are gone from us. Perhaps like you they think of us as crap. No doubt they are right. Crap.

Over disastrous road-works the vehicles crawled and skidded and bounced. He turned the radio on again. An advertisement for something called a Dance In The Dark. Introduced breathlessly by someone, mock-London Cockney accent of course, which the kids admired these days, dumber the better, named Whammer. He turned the radio off. His house, and the red-tiled roofs of others just like it, swung round like a modest flotilla on the mucky green horizon and cars swung right and left off the main road, going home.

'Do you not feel funny out here, talking to me?'

He gave it a moment's thought. Off in the cool evening sea a filthy-looking cargo boat jogged towards the docks. The wharfs were empty these days; he remembered boats from the islands, a cow suspended in mid air, screaming as a crude mechanism swung her off the deck and on to the shit-spattered quay.

41

And the thick black coal-dust mottling the air, the yelps of Polish sailors, pale-faced, leaning over their ship's rails smoking.

Dockers went down to the ships in the wee dark hours, nerving themselves against the lurking Customs officers, coming off the ships with bottles of Polish brandy, vodka and cheap cigarettes. He couldn't think of the boy when he remembered, looking at the lazy cargo vessel sprawled on the blue pillows of the far hills, the dead joy of his own boyhood.

Seagulls circled and toughed it out noisily on the rising breeze. Couples walked past. Teenagers on skate-boards rattled on, turned, rattled on again. Girls walked by in their crotch-hugging, wind-blown skirts. He looked at their moulded cloth triangles, he looked at the lines of their underwear as they disappeared up the promenade. He felt an odd sense of scratchy peace. He came to himself.

'Not a bit, really.'

'Well, I would,' said the boy. 'Supposing someone recognises you?'

'So what?'

'Well, then, supposing someone recognises me, and sees you talking to me....'

There was wisdom in that. And a spot of caring. The boy liked him, was it possible? Liked him enough to make him aware. Out of the mouths of babes and all that.

But he'd been lonely and now he wasn't anymore. He had someone to talk to. He didn't expect anyone to understand that but they could bugger off. They'd think the other thing, of course. He wasn't about to explain himself. The boy was not attractive in any way, God save us, it wasn't like that. He was a tramp, sniffly, drank when he could get it, maybe fifteen or so, smoked like a train. But from the moment the boy had sat down on the bench in the half-light, the sad smoky blue light that comes off the sea when the bay's calm and the voices of the men fishing off the rocks sounds all the way down in the breeze; from that moment, when he'd asked the boy to stay where he was, even as the boy made to get up, wasting his time, no sale, he'd been aware. Aware, terribly, of the hole in himself. Into which he plunged, feeling a first sadness, but it was less than a tug at the heart's shirt hanging out.

The boy hadn't seemed as if he'd wanted to go off anyway. He'd been tired. He'd been hungry. Nothing in taking the boy for a burger and chips. A coffee in a paper cup, too hot to lift up, to drink. It had seemed like an adventure. He could talk and talk. The boy didn't say much but their meeting had been enough, a beginning, if you like. He wanted to talk forever, tell the boy who he really was. And tell him about the book. Not like father to son, that's rubbish. Or man to man, the boy was too young. Something else.

43

When finally the boy had said he was leaving, then he'd done the appalling thing. Then he'd handed him the fiver. Just to sit a little longer and listen.

He stopped the car, engine running, and looked, amazed as he always was, at the rough white two-storey houses with their red roofs, all gleaming in the late sinking sun, all the same. There was something sullen and bashful about them, as if they were never meant to be lived in, as if to open their doors was to violate them. They stood cowering in the dirty fields, the brown rock shore, the stone-and-water timelessness of everything around them. The builder's advertising hoarding was still up, though by now, rained upon, blasted with salt wind, it hung and flapped like a colourful bird with an injured wing. Rain had darkened the heaps of earth, the earth-embedded wooden timbers, that still sat and lay in front or to the side of the new houses. He drove off now and his tyres smoothed down in light toppings of chocolate mud.

She was out in the garden, he could see her through the open back door. The garden smelled of new turned earth and grass. She bent over, stooping to some task beyond him. The red message indicator on their phone blinked and blinked suggestively. She never answered the phone these days, as if nothing good could come of letting the mysterious world whisper in your ear. So he pressed the button. The whispering crackle and crash was of a mobile phone in a car. He listened, bent slightly over the phone as if it were a small animal under his hungry, birdy eye.

'Just remembered, but you'd left.'

The slightest hint that he'd left the damned job before he should have done. But he'd left on time, he knew that. He hated that someone's tone of voice could insert a quiver of fear in him, a child scolded.

'Hold on. I'm driving. Traffic lights. Now. If we could meet earlier than what we said, say around tennish. I'd be obliged, means I can get away to Dublin before lunchtime. The rest of them I'll phone when I get home now. See you then.'

The throbbing tone, signing off, then the quick pips. The red light stopped flashing. The change of time frightened him. That things could change like that, there had to be a reason, not just getting off earlier to Dublin. He hated himself, thinking, feeling like this. A grown man. This was the way things worked these days. Priorities changed all the time. He stood up, looked around a sitting room still smelling faintly of drying cement. Behind the pictures, the paper, under the carpets, under the witheringly-expensive leather couch and armchairs, the house was drying out and settling. Contracting. Closing in.

He retreated upstairs to his novel. The screen flashed and scrolled and opened the file. He was hungry, but the urge to see the words again overcame his hunger. When the black Roman lettering appeared, he relaxed, as if they wormed under his skin, fed his blood. He felt the sense of the words, the world he was creating. There was a logic here. And he controlled what happened next. The formation of his story gave him a sense of power he felt he lacked in what passed for the real world, he'd be the first to admit that. Not to her, of course, she wouldn't understand.

The boy did. It didn't have to be said. He'd mentioned the novel and the boy's nodding was enough. Under the arcade lights, the fat, elderly, lonely Bingo signs in the window. When they'd played the machines, the boy winning once or twice, whatever winning meant in there. The boy looking like his son and the wine-haired young girl, student perhaps, ring in her nose, reading her Thackeray behind the plastic window of the pay-out booth, not caring one way or the other, not asking about his age, not even looking up.

The machines played their madhouse scramble of musical notes and the symbols came up, never in line; he knew it would be possible to work out mathematical odds and that sort of thing. He played his machine thirty-two times in a row before he earned ten points in green numerals on a digital display. Around him, in the odour of sweat and smoke and stale carpets, under the twinkling eye of closed-circuit cameras, lonely, badly-dressed women smoked and coveted their machines hungrily. Some played two machines at a time, hands flickering like icy birds back

46

and forth, back and forth. A rancid, smoky smell hung in the air. The noise in the place was terrific, a metallic sing-song, a rattle of numbers and chance and coin, and the argument of frustrated gamblers.

The boy moved to the poker machines. He seemed to know something about them, the way he sat into it. The great thing about being in here was you never had to speak. He watched the boy, watched him electronically turn his cards, heard his soft curses.

He counted the number of words in his novel. He'd read somewhere that a particular total constituted a legitimate novel, so many made a short story, and so on. He was aiming for one-hundred-thousand, which he considered was pretty good. He felt good every time he finished and saved what he'd written. Overcoming something, a victory. Not the sort of thing you'd talk about in work; but then there was nothing you'd talk about in work. So many things were forbidden in that world. He began to write, elaborating, fleshing out, as they said, one of his main characters, a woman.

He'd read about ways of writing about women. Dress up as a woman while writing? Ha-Ha! Well, no. Talk to her in the garden? Ask her things? What is it like to be you? A dangerous question. No. He worked on, going well, then becoming confused. Tired. But the tiredness seemed to come from somewhere very far within. It wasn't physical fatigue. It felt like something shifting laboriously inside his heart. When he looked at

47

the screen he could not understand anything he had written. His woman character evaded him.

The boy had nodded, seeming to understand. It was more than possible that he did, he wasn't an uneducated lad. Circumstances do things to us all, bring us to where we are, make us. We are not responsible. The arcade had tired them both. Outside, it had begun to rain and he felt guilty and furtive. The boy said he knew where to find him: no, he'd replied, let's make a more definite arrangement, I hate uncertainties.

There was the odour of frying. It cloyed its way into his room. He printed out the very first chapter, closed down, switched things off.

At the kitchen table, no radio on, no TV, the silence in the rooms speckled with the odd sound of something tweeting in the garden, he spoke to his wife in small tones about nothing in particular. She told him about a woman she knew, an old neighbour, who'd found a lump in her breast. Mouth full of bacon well sauced, he wanted to say Do you think she could find me one? but he just ran the phrase through his head and chewed on, nodding. She spoke, then, of tests and worry. Then she said she supposed she should start worrying, her age, any age really, about things like that herself.

Then she impaled a sausage, cut it in half, asked him whether a fry was enough for him, just that'd she'd been in the garden all day and was tired, or did he want something more? He brought his back teeth down on a very hot chip, it was burning his tongue, his jaw. He reached quickly for water but she hadn't poured any. When he swallowed he could feel the thing burning his gullet. It would be sore when he swallowed later, he'd imagine throat cancer. She got up, went to the sink, came back with a glass of water, but it was too late. Across the cluttered table, she smelled of sweat and something he couldn't pin down.

Her age. She smells of her age. As I must, he told himself. Age has a smell. That's it.

They had instant coffee, but it said on the label that it came from Havana, so she'd bought it, he knew, for what it said on the label.

'Helen is coming over.'

'When?'

'Easter. With a friend.'

'A boyfriend?'

'I suppose so. Do you mind?'

No, he didn't mind. Helen was, besides, good fun. His favourite, and probably his other kids knew it. Helen was tall, gangly, attractive and funny. It was not a bad combination. He thought about the woman character in his novel. She lacked humour. She could be a bit more like Helen, a bit more daughterly, come to that. But she was too old in the story.

They'll try not to fuck, at least not loudly, he

49

thought. So's they wake us up. He couldn't imagine what it would be like to hear his daughter moaning in sexual ecstasy through the bedroom walls. He thought about it, and odd feelings flushed through him, from the knees up. A sort of pins and needles but not very pleasant. When he thought of something else, they receded. But a guilty anger remained, and it took time to go away.

He thought of the boy, of showing him, at last, the novel, a chapter at least, reading it to him or letting him read it. It didn't matter, in fact it would be nicer to have the boy come back with a criticism, say something from an outside point of view, as it were. Was it too strong for the boy? No, not these days, kids weren't really kids anymore. The videos they had at their disposal, after all. Violence and black ghetto language. And sex and drugs. Common currency to the young. But he was right to at least think of these things, and he felt good, fatherly, that he'd considered the boy, his feelings, his emotions. The coffee was going cold. All the way from Havana. Fidel Castro. Fat cigars. Was it really true, or just a story, that the CIA'd put explosives in some of his cigars but he'd caught on?

'They'll be sleeping together in the one room.'

He heard his wife's voice but it came from somewhere else, not from her, not from inside this room. He buttered a triangle of toast messily and, cutting a segment free, used it to wipe up the yellow and brown grease-mess on his plate. He saw the way the bread, wiping, left regular trails like the marks of a plough over a snowy field; he saw that the plate was cracked, a jagged bolt of lightning from one side to the other, the crack was hair thin. He could think of nothing to reply to his wife. Some things were said and then the words evaporated, dissolved in the heat of disinterest. Dissolved in the heat of disinterest wasn't a bad phrase. He could use that. The woman in his story would be well read as well as beautiful. She would have an interest in music and poetry. She could debate with the best of them.

He took his cup out to the front door and once there, smoked a cigarette. She disliked him smoking, it left an after-smell, she said, coining a phrase with bitterness; you'll smell up the house. He'd smoked occasionally for years and she'd never objected, smoked herself now and then. Now it was another bone upon which, it seemed to him, she chewed contentedly. He smoked, felt the first drowsy nervousness of the nicotine, the speeding up of his heart. He hadn't figured out a title for his book and he thought, with the boy's help, one would come. The boy lived the way he lived. He threw the cigarette out onto the ridged, uneven cement path. The wind rolled it over and over, back and forth.

Dishes piled at futuristic angles in the silvery sink, the odour of hot water and green detergent creeping

51

like a poisoned gas through the rooms; he watched her pull on big manly garden gloves and shuffle out again. We seek life in strange places, he thought to himself, watching her bending back. If he were a painter, that's how he would paint her, bending, like Van Gogh had done with women just like her, in a field, toiling to inject new life into dull dark earth. He remembered a couple of lines, no more, of an old poem from his schooldays:

> 'I and Pangur Bán, my cat
> 'Tis a like task we are at....'

He thought of how a poem could be composed out of her working in the garden and his working to cultivate words. He looked at his wife, her back bending and straightening, her absorption in her task, the grunt of her breath when she straightened, the way she flicked her rakish brown hair out of her eyes when she bent over again. Over her head on a washing line hung a couple of his fishnet vests and one of her slips, light blue, a line of sad cold-coloured signal-flags flicking helplessly to no one.

The television news bored him, tribunals for this and that, no one would ever see the inside of a jail and that's all we know for certain; he shifted from channel to channel, looking for something interesting, anything, really, to stop the increasing rotations of his mind.

I will work forever, until I die, he thought; I do not know even where the Cayman Islands might be found on a map. I have never been to the Isle of Man. I have never visited Dublin Castle. He looked for a few minutes at a ladies' tennis match, but they didn't do those luscious bum-shots, the frilled tight white knickers, anymore. Untouchable, unreachable women. Behind the safe glass of the screen. No way in. He received an image, halfway between the TV screen and his eyes, hanging out in that space, of his daughter with her legs open and it unsteadied him so much that he shook his head and emitted a tiny, feminine whine. He stood up abruptly, switching the set off as he rose to his feet. A lightness blew over his skull, a dizziness.

A grey-blue colour covered the roads, the fields darkening, some lights coming on. The first chapter of the novel sat beside him brightly on the passenger seat. He smoked freely in the car, opened the window, smelled the evening air, the sun locked down now behind low clouds over the Atlantic Ocean. Above him, miles into the blue-dark page of sky, two white pencil lines traced for him where a jet made its insect path towards the New World.

He drove beside the calm bay. The tide was out, children galloped in the low light along the soft wormy sand, dark unhuman figures in a dull landscape of wet sand and receding water. Thin slices, like a Japanese painting. On his car radio, Robert Johnson playing

Come On In My Kitchen. The Blues, when you sold your soul to the devil, sounded like this. There was a sound you made when you were condemned. He remembered how cool it had seemed among his university pals way back in the days of thunder to have a black girlfriend. Exotic. Like a beautiful ebony bangle, a watchstrap. Nothing to do with anything else. He moved away roughly now when black women pushed past him, different and therefore dangerous, with their children in colourful buggies. All over the place. Not my place anymore. Wrong thinking, but can't be helped. I am what I am.

The radio presenter was telling the nipped, robbed life of Robert Johnson, using an accent he'd never heard before, not Irish, English, not anything. Neutral, between nowhere and nowhere. You could get like that, not knowing where or who. Or what it was, this thing that made you you. He wanted to get out of the car and walk the promenade, be the same as everybody else and go home, disappear into their disappearing; the brisk walks of the middle-aged women, their chattering breathlessly as they went by, rigid and ridiculous. A lone woman with a yappy dog on a lead. A young man on a bench drinking from a fat plastic bottle. Night coming on.

The boy found him, it was just like that. He'd parked the car and moved himself and his heart into a comfortable position and he'd walked, manuscript under his arm, like any university man out for a stroll and some salt air, a few hundred yards along the promenade, meeting no one he knew, beginning to feel let down. When the boy had appeared from nowhere, up out of the ground, as it were, white collar grubby, ripped runners unlaced, he looked worse, that is more vulnerable, than ever. The boy's appearance of vulnerability was an affront, a threat. Manuscript under his arm still, he steered them quickly along the promenade so that they didn't stick out, standing talking, being aware all over again.

On the near black horizon, under the fat humped mountains across the bay, a vague ship slouched out towards the islands, under the stare of Black Head. It seemed not to be moving at all. As he walked, a salted breeze blew up, full of fine grains of sand, off the revealed, drying beach. Black weeded rocks showed like bad teeth in an enormous mouth. He felt the breeze on his face, let it sound a note or two in his ear.

My father took me here, just like this, walking with a boy his age, we watched on bright evenings as the year fell away the thin fishermen's rods whip and thread out and through the moist air, and I envied the boys who sat with their fathers on the rocks and hooked bait. He'd buy me ice-cream and we'd watch from a distance, from here, on the promenade, as if he imagined I might do something to myself so close to the water, he nodding, grunting a greeting with no

emotion in it, nothing, at men who did the same to
him as they went by.

'Have you cigarettes?'

'Yes, I have.'

He gave the boy a cigarette and lighted it for him,
their faces too close, their breaths almost touching, as in
cupped hands they saved the flame. A small fat girl on
skates flung past them, her chubby bottom straining in
blue shorts, fat thighs whispering together, she
disappeared into the accumulating gloom, a sudden
splash of buxom colour, then gone. He flicked the match
flame out, threw away the burnt stick, saw, as he raised
his head, the ugly yellowness of the front of a gigantic
hotel, a brick ship, sailing slowly in its stubborn tide of
gravel and grass. I can't remember what was there
before it, he thought. I can't think at all.

They sat on a cold wooden green bench which had
two slats missing so that your backside hurt to sit back on
it. He wanted to show the boy the manuscript right away,
yet there was something more in savouring the moment.

The boy smoked, blew grey smoke into the air
where it vanished frantically. For a long time the boy
stared out over the dark bay, you could see stubble on
his chin, a child's first stubble, then the flakes of scalp
in his thick hair, like dirty snow or bits of paint. Where
do you live? But he had never asked that question, it
presumed too much, too pointed, not in his game. He
allowed the boy his cigarette. Time passed in the

breeze and he counted people walking by, some going left, some right, some walking quickly, some crouched over, walking as if in a dream. There were strangers here and people he knew. A shopkeeper here, a young schoolteacher there, giggling in her schoolgirlishness, a schoolgirl always. And there he saw an old mayor of the town. Got very decrepit, he thought; and creaks, limps, like a man with a bad hip. Oh.

'I have to be somewhere in a while,' said the boy, not looking at him.

'Oh. Well, then.'

His disappointment welled up like indigestion. A quaint windy disorder below his ribs, moving outwards. Like fear. But not fear. He countered quickly.

'There's something I've been intending to show you,' he said, making it light, lifting his voice out of the bottom of his throat. The boy looked at him. His eyes were red, lack of sleep, and something else, a wariness, he'd heard everything that could be said a thousand times, maybe it all started off like this.

'What?'

A blunt, slow word, said slowly, barely a question at all. He felt the boy's blank eyes on him and all of a sudden, angry from nowhere, he was reluctant to show the boy anything, to reveal this manuscript, what he'd worked on for so long, the thing that, God knows, kept him sane half the time. Not to be dismissed raggedly by a kid, a street-kid, like this.

'You're not interested. There's no point, in that case.'

The manuscript squeezed itself page by page, a little cowering timorous beastie now, against his hot chest.

'Huh.'

The boy didn't care. It was like love rebuked. Now he was staring back out to the bay and the sullen ship, out of sight, almost, and had turned on tiny pricks of light in the dark, one of them blinking faintly blue like a distant planet. He saw her bending Van Gogh back in the garden, the plump gloves too big, too floundering, too male for her; he saw her hands, not ungentle, never that, but dried and pinched, the skin folding thickly, crevassing, as she brought the lightning-forked plate to the table. A bottle of YR sauce in a cupboard, a green egg cup she'd made herself in a pottery class years ago; images of things, you could long for only these things in all the world. As you could desire, feverishly like a madman, a familiar newspaper or an old shirt. Exiled from them, out in the foreign land of one step behind yourself.

'Well, I'll show it to you anyway, even if you don't appreciate it.'

Said lightly again, a garnish of regret to make the boy's eyes fall ground-wards, to insert a twinge of guilt. But the boy stood up, sighing like a leaf falling, and stood over him. The crotch of the boy's trousers was stained, map-like, little empires of love-making or what passed for it.

Sadness, now, no mistaking it. And a cold sense of having acted foolishly, but for a long time, not just in recent days, but for a long time stretching back to his swaddling days. He had the manuscript out now, its pages flicking over in the breeze, it looked and felt ridiculous, like a paper plea. He stood up too because there was nothing else to do and he'd caught side-eyed the curious glances of the walkers and stumblers. The boy talking down to the man, father and son arguing, but they don't look like father and son, not really, look closer.

Now standing over the boy again, he prepared to be led by him. It was dark now, high orange promenade lights chinked on, the place turned a strange science-fiction colour and the flesh on the boy's face turned strange too, as if the texture was different, putty perhaps, soap. I should go home, he thought; now, while there's still time. Dignity. He felt his own loneliness and was amazed by it, he wanted to study it, prick it apart strand by strand. Where had it all come from? Where had it begun? Where born, whither going? The boy turned away, said something under his breath. He trotted a few steps and caught up.

'What did you say? I didn't hear you.'

'I have to be somewhere.'

He felt the ground change under his feet, its gritty solidness replaced by the soft green of the grass. They were moving over the road, not much traffic this hour, they walked faster, too fast, the damned manuscript flapping in his hand, it must look absurd, a nutty professor pursuing an errant student, something out of a Bolton Brothers comedy, black-and-white, the old days. The Estoria cinema was demolished, something new, fast, in its place. It should have been Astoria, but no one had bothered to make a correction, it was spelled the way people said the word, that was it. Upstairs on Sunday nights, smoking with your legs up on the balcony rail, the projected film always slanted for some reason and a portion of it thrown off the screen and onto the wall. Where he had courted her, her dress sliding up, take the back row this time. Don't, she used to say. Don't. Like a child.

The coloured lights of the amusement arcade dripped and dappled on the parchment-dry pavement, empty cigarette cartons and rolled-up potato-crisp packets and hamburger wrappers cartwheeled into the gutters. A pint glass half-filled with stale piss-coloured beer sat fatly on a ledge beside a cash point in the wall of a bank. Out of the take-away cafés and the Chinese restaurants rolled the smell of cooking. Early yet, later the women for the Bingo would come, descending waddle-hipped and sexless from the ugly hired bus.

The boy was making for the amusement arcade, so it seemed, but he didn't want to go there, it was too bloody early, this was absurd. This lack of control.

This running after a boy. He said:

'Look, where exactly are you taking me?'

The boy stopped, looked at him sternly. Now there was in the boy's face an older thing, a dangerous thing. He hadn't seen anything like it before. The world was there, the boy's acquired world, and he was no match, no match.

He felt his feet step back one step, two.

'I want a coffee,' the boy said, and he grinned and walked off past the arcade, the coloured lights pouring over him. He disappeared into a fast-food café.

The boy had already ordered. The paper-hatted young girl, beautiful in a round-faced way, could barely speak English. Two coffees appeared, too hot to drink, to carry. The place was empty, plastic music played out of the high wall speakers, songs full of lovely safe anguish, sterilised delicious hurt, aimed at teenagers. They sat down, sat in to, red plastic seats. For a little while they said nothing, just stirred their coffee with plastic sticks that were not, could never be, as efficient as spoons. There were shouts from somewhere behind the dugout of gleaming silvery fryers, a girl's throaty laugh.

'So, what is it?'

He took up the manuscript, the boy had noticed it, of course, hard not to, knew its importance and had dismissed its mystery. His question contained no curiosity. No warmth at all. He sipped at his coffee.

The boy was facing him, facing the entrance, the plastic glass doors, the street.

'This. It's the novel. I told you I was doing it. I wanted you to be the first to see it.'

He shoved the chapter across the chilly red vinyl table-top. White grains of salt were wedged around its edges. The boy turned the pages round to him, looked at the first paragraph, moved his eyes over it too quickly. The boy would not understand, of course he wouldn't, what effort had gone into it, what it meant, really meant, behind what it meant. He saw her bending again, away from him, unconnected to him, not knowing him, the plants and grasses greeting her motherly trowelling, her loving probing. And the meeting for the morning rescheduled and hanging like a poisonous vapour in his head if he thought about it, like those images of his daughter, unbidden, deadly, what you couldn't think about too much, what it all indicated, or you'd go mad.

'Are you reading it?'

'I know how to read,' the boy said, not looking up. His eyes moved over the lines too quickly, nervously, for that matter. He turned a page, grimaced at something, snorted, sipped his coffee, not taking his eyes of the page, which was good. A good sign. Perhaps it would be possible to discuss the thing with the boy, if the boy thought to ask a question, perhaps, take it from there.

'Well?'

'I'm reading.'

'Do you understand it?'

'Not all of it.'

Perhaps that meant he couldn't read after all. Street-kid, he never talked about himself like that, his parents.

'You never talk about your parents.'

'Don't you want me to read this for you?'

Yes, he thought; read it for me. That's what it is, really. A favour. Paid for, or will be; how much to read my manuscript? He was angry again, not at the bay, not at himself, just at the way things could be, sitting in a sad take-away in the in-between hours when no one was out in the streets yet, not really, not yet ready for going out, sitting at home preparing. Having something to prepare for. The Estoria. The flicking images on the side wall. A magic-lantern of a place in your head.

'Where do you have to go this evening?'

'Nowhere special.'

The boy kept reading. There was so little to say when you thought you had lots to say. Nothing was like a novel, a movie. Everything was like real life.

'I'll make a deal with you.'

The boy's eyes this way and that over the pages, he couldn't have been reading them. Now, finally, he raises his head from the curled rampant pages of the first chapter of his novel, the novel whose main woman character he cannot define as he wishes to just yet, and he's looking over his shoulder out into the street where you can hear people walking if you listen.

'What sort of a deal?'

'I want you to read that chapter and tell me what you think of it. Honestly. And I'll pay you for your time and expertise.'

The boy sniggered. A dirty sound, a ratty back alley of a sound, with your trousers down. He saw the boy then, a different boy, a new boy. And saw himself and felt the two fivers in his fingers.

'I think it's shit,' the boy said, sitting back.

'I want you to take it home with you and read it carefully. You can't have read it carefully, now.'

Stepping off, floating almost, he saw her below him, very far away, lift her face from the earth and stare upwards into the sun, shielding her eyes, the hair falling back from her face, earth under her fingernails. The white houses sat gleaming all around her like well-tended tombs.

'You're crazy.'

The boy looked up, saying something else without making any sound, the two fivers in his hand, he'd taken the money anyway as I knew he would, couldn't resist it, it's what he does. He reached over, tired suddenly, wanting his manuscript back, the money didn't matter.

The boy stood up.

They took the manuscript out of his hands, they were almost tender about it. He felt a power under his arm, lifting him upwards, so he had to shift out of the seat, it was awkward. They were standing everywhere, they were like big black birds. Their faces shone on him, glowing with an irrefutable power.

The kitchen staff came out to look, knew without any doubt what they were looking at, turned shy, sniping glances at the man from behind their swept trench between the counter and the fryers. The car was outside, parked with ugly precision right in front of the entrance. People passed by, looked in, kept going. Nothing like this mattered. A metallic voice clattered through a radio.

'What are you doing?' he managed to say. His voice was clogged with nervous phlegm.

The boy had moved out of the seating and was standing with one of them; he'd taken the two fivers out of the boy's fingers. The other one who had the manuscript was flipping through the pages.

'Juicy stuff,' this one said.

An ignorant man, he thought, to be reading my manuscript, not in the least comprehending what he reads. A stupid man.

'It's shit,' the boy said. He wasn't sniggering now, just looking, looking and growing fainter and fainter until he was a mere ghost, had never been there,

65

something he'd made up.

'What are you doing with me?'

They'd turned him round, seen it all before, the first question, one on either side, a sort of march, almost a weary dutiful familiarity in it, as if they'd rehearsed themselves for just this event. Or others like it.

The boy had disappeared; well, he'd never been real, had he? Sometimes you know when a thing isn't real, but you keep it to yourself.

It was, however, of the utmost importance that he was in good shape, thinking clearly, for the meeting. She'd be waiting up in bed with the light on reading something, she always was. And she'd ask him what he had on, a habit of hers, didn't mean anything, for the following day. A ritual, reassured her, irritated him. He'd tell her tiredly. But it was amazing right now how you couldn't find anything to say, things moved too quickly, a clever choreography to them, a ritual of their own, went ahead of you and away from you. He was aware, but it was different now.

A big hand rested firmly on the back of his head and pushed him downwards so that he ducked whether he wanted to or not climbing in to the back seat. The door was closed behind him, there was no handle on the inside. He looked back quickly and saw the girl who'd served them standing watching from the entrance to the take-away and her round face expressionless until it faded out in the dark and distance.

The one in the front beside the driver had the manuscript now. He was reading, his head down, the neat line of haircut and the white back of the neck, half-hearted street light clipping the silver numbers on his shoulders. They were big men, one either side of him in the back seat. The pages of his manuscript looked violated, guilty. The car gathered speed, moaned forward.

The bay was there and then it was gone.

# Collateral Damage

'...but I had more to do than spend all day resuscitating fish when I had meals to prepare for humans.'

Bernadette Mulligan: *Full Military Honours*

It took all day.

Even when it was over, nothing looked over.

When she'd given back the key, crossed the dead gravel space under the gashed children's slide and the destroyed swings and handed the key to a man who stepped up from a table where they were playing poker, asked her if she could read the sign, look, there, on the wall, and that all complaints had to be made directly to City Hall; even when she'd told him she wasn't making a complaint but handing back her key and they kept on playing with their blue overalled backs to her, the stale tea and cigarettes ooze of the place; it was a moment or two before this humped snarling rat of a man got up and approached her. Even with the door of that dead flat locked permanently and the silent breathless dusty space inside no longer hers or her son's or anybody's, she felt the unsettling push of great earth-deep machines. Hard cogs, ratchets, slippery pistons.

The Corporation man, who lacked good manners or any kind of grace, eyed her up and down, took the key.

'Right.'

He went back to his poker game, pocketing the key. Maybe he'd slip a relative in to the flat before it was cold. He had the face for it, a world-meanness.

Some of them were sniggering and looking at her legs even though she was wearing jeans. Behind her, over the blocks of flats, a broken exhaust made a car engine sound like a tractor. The walls of the structures had once been white; salt in the wind had streaked them red and pink, you could step on a needle here or there in the wrecked thin grass, young lads were thugs. TV dishes sat out like mouths over the balconies, you could hear daytime programmes and the odd blue movie groan sweep down from the windows.

When Darren screwed her he kept one hand lightly pressed over her mouth because her gasp and shout embarrassed him. He imagined everyone had an ear to the thin walls, he always bit his tongue when he came, trying to keep himself noiseless. You could hear the beatings scrabbling up from the floor downstairs too, some woman screaming and the dog yapping and his swearing. It was not like in films or in books. The misery up here was what your imagination did with scraps of this and that. You couldn't get this second-hand, like going to the Simon Shop and taking it off a hanger, no.

Someone's rubbish spun upwards in a sort of widening visual poetry, like a piece of metal sculpture she'd seen in school, pages from men's magazines with busty girls nude and some of the pages brownly stained as they lifted off into the air off the gravel and round and round as she walked away. She grabbed the buggy handles and pushed and Jackie twitched a little and squealed and they moved off. The child's nose was running, the sun was hot, there was dust and dirty magazines in the air, there was the smell of hot engine oil and food frying and the teenagers moping, trying to look cool and hard and looking silly in baggy trousers and turn-round cheap baseball caps spitting all the time from their throats to look harder and menacing as they'd seen someone do in a Yank film or on TV. Or outside a betting-office. Or in a pub.

She folded the buggy while the taxi-driver held Jackie, who protested and flapped her thick short legs in her fat, hot nappy. Everything else had gone ahead, there was nothing but herself and the folded buggy in the car's boot and her daughter smelling now in the heat of the taxi and the radio playing, a programme host making his voice drop, drop until it was the same level and tone as the woman caller whose real mother she'd just met for the very first time. And how did you feel?

Sometimes radio or TV or newspaper people had visited the flats, but they'd never interviewed her and they'd avoided the middle-aged man living alone in the top flat who listened to Classical music and wrote book reviews on the side, with his dole and poetry too, and they'd interviewed always and always the family on the opposite side of the playground, she was piggishly fat and he was always having court orders against him to stay away, but she'd always take him back and they with their six kids – two of them someone else's, not his – were celebrities because they knew how to suffer well on camera and in front tape-recorders. Suffering brought viewers and listeners.

And still she would read that other man's book reviews every Saturday in a national newspaper and see his poems, some of which she'd cut out and kept, meaning to frame someday, and no one ever bothered to interview him about the place or her, whose boyfriend, Jackie's father, was a soldier doing his duty serving his country. There was the life you lived and the life the TV wanted to see and they were different.

The taxi drove down the long road she'd walked up often with Jackie when she was even younger and couldn't even fit in a buggy and she was aware of Jackie's smell and the smell of her own clothes which most of the time was cigarettes. The flat had been small and one window was jammed shut and the Corporation had told her they weren't responsible for damage done by herself in the flat but she hadn't, the window had just jammed and they wouldn't fix it and she hadn't the money and neither had Darren. The Corpo, she'd been told by older women, will not do a thing for you. You have to take that from the first.

It was true. They had no respect for people in the flats. They were all related, that's how they got and kept their jobs. The town thought it was big and sophisticated and growing because the Dublin papers said so, but it was really still a village and everyone lived up your arse, knew your business.

The taxi turned where the thatched cottages used to be, thatch yellow in the summer sun and the whitewash white and refreshing and they'd put slate roofs on because, someone had written to the paper, a preservation order couldn't be put on them and then next thing the two lovely houses were gone, demolished over a weekend. There were letters in the local paper, but the Corporation only pretended to be angry and no one was ever prosecuted.

Now blocky, shoe-boxy structures were going up, grey breeze-block by breeze-block, ask the students any kind of rent they'll pay it. And the Romanians and Nigerians and Indians and all the rest will pay what they're asked. There were politicians in this town who owned flats and nothing was ever said. 'There were buildings went up,' Dad said, 'that defied every regulation you could think of, look at the height of some of them, and one or two of those responsible got roof apartments out of it; they could investigate themselves and find nothing all they liked. Every cat dog and divil knows.'

Her Mam said you couldn't go around accusing people just like that and her Dad said what about that man who was after the young lads and everyone knew about that and half the town knew who he was too and the police said in the papers they'd looked and wouldn't be prosecuting, well known he wasn't working class, some big knob. Her Mam laughed shyly and her Dad was annoyed at himself for saying something that might be construed as funny and therefore ruining his point.

Her Mam always reflected in the light from the kitchen window, the radio always on. Her Dad with a newspaper, her brothers washed, shaved, out, gone hours ago. But now her Dad would be at the house, and he was, with her brother James, the only one on the dole, thank God, and the taxi had taken the short cut by the hospital instead of going down the West where the out-of-towners – hippies – had taken over the pubs, her Dad declared from an armchair. No one from the town ever goes there, which wasn't true. But her Dad used a different map when he talked about the town. Older, from the time he was born.

The taxi drew up, there they were. Furniture, what there was of it, bits of this and that, like objects blown into her life rather than purchased; her Dad panting and acting like a boss of something, James in tight white vest showing off his unworked muscles to God knew who, the houses small and bright and white and red-roofed in the grey light. The woman at the door greeted her reluctantly, you could smell that, the hesitation, then the anger for no reason at all, the voice.

'Just sign your name here, if you please.'

And she signed her name on the clipboard sheet, saw the other names, scrawls, one or two who couldn't write. One hand on the pen, the other wrapped around Jackie, under her arse, the smell of her hot and horrible.

'Follow me.'

The woman was as old as her Mam, better dressed, a suit of blue, heels that clack-clacked as the sun went in and out bitterly; the sound of a chair scraping concrete, James swearing, the removal van like a snarling animal, the engine still on, the driver doing nothing. The woman moved fat-arsed up the concrete cream pathway, still dry cement and filler in the small garden, in through the gleaming blue door, pushing; the door didn't hang properly. Inside the house the bareness and the cold and the smell of concrete and the empty space of the rooms stopped her breath like a sad pollen. She wanted to put Jackie down somewhere on the floor, clean her up, nappies in her bag, but the woman kept walking full of her impatience, moving

75

from room to empty room, making her anxious, filling the little house with authority and threat and danger, no welcome, she wouldn't rise to that.

'Here's a tenant's handbook. No lodgers, no late-night parties, no parking caravans or anything else out in the garden, no pets, you are not allowed to renovate or build on extensions without first notifying us first. All complaints about structural work must be made before the end of...'

Resenting, resenting, the woman could hardly hold herself back. Where did she come from that this is power to her, me standing here with a filthy baby and wanting to change her nappy, in my new house? When the woman moved away, sleek her car and silvery blue, the air remained full of her, of her hard words and the sound of her voice, a landlady's voice, pisses perfume, penny looking down on a halfpenny.

'I know her brother,' her Dad said, passing with armfuls of chair. 'A docker. Drinks his wage-packet.'

Carrying, trailing this listed information like a victory banner after him as he walked hunched up the path into the house, struggling to angle the chair around the door, she looked at her nails on her free hand, red-painted from something or somewhere, chipped, and she was biting them like when she was a kid in school she'd pick her nose from nerves. What her Dad was saying was don't worry.

She changed Jackie's nappy on the concrete chilled

floor of the empty sitting-room, James looking down screwing up his face, the smell of her for the size of her, he said. Here, and she handed him the full hot nappy like a soggy bag of chips to get rid of. He swore at her but not angrily and disappeared with it.

Then there was laughter outside. The street was hers, she owned it now, no-one else there, she the first in a house. The rows of new white houses squatted innocent and fragile on the big green space where the Summer circus used to draw in, their growling coloured trucks and a fluttering marquee every year. Where the old woman half mad had gone to feed the lions and had her arm chewed off. A court-case, all the town sitting in the galleries.

Hot hard high weeds lingered at the side nearest the dual carriageway, the roundabout where the cars went too fast and getting across with a buggy would be impossible, she'd said so on the first trip out here, her Mam saying if you turn this house down you'll never get another, they'll put you down the list.

And the houses, she had to admit, looked nice. Bits of gardens, full of rocks and occasional grass, you could bend down and pick up a piece of broken crockery, as if in some of those television Geographic films, you were excavating a Roman villa in Spain. New houses, the fields upturned, meant rats but they'd go away if they existed at all, it was normal, said her father. A rat won't do you any harm, scared of humans.

77

She took out smaller things that she could handle with one eye on Jackie and put them about, no nails in the walls, the woman had said but, how else would you hang a picture? She took out a silly fat glass rainbow-coloured fish that Darren had won at the amusements when she was just pregnant last year by throwing three small footballs into a bucket and they stayed there. She put the mouth-open ugly thing and heavy too up on the little cement-dusted shelf above the fireplace, a great thing to have, a real fire. When she opened a window, double-glazed, the lock stiff, strange-feeling in her hand, she inhaled the earthy sexual tang of tall damp grass.

The rooms still wore emptiness like a shawl, mourning old women cluttered together, but they brightened up with a few chairs and a bed inside them. Jackie crawled and grunted. Her Dad came in, James came in, going and coming with boxes and items of furniture, you never could tell when they'd come in handy, everything. She tried turning on the electric cooker after her Dad had connected it to the electric, wouldn't work so he tried again and Be careful! she shouted at him when he was especially in behind the cooker amid the wires with his pliers. Jackie she had to keep an eye on too. When they left, the sound of the rooms moving in and out breathing like an infant finding its lungs was a whisper like rain in her ears but it wasn't and she thought she was hearing things.

She made tea and toast and sat watching the grainy snow-falling TV screen, she'd have to get an aerial. 'I'll fix you up with something,' James had said, but he was always promising and she didn't want to be caught for a licence she couldn't afford Court. She liked Coronation Street. Even through the blizzard of a million million waves and bands and broadcasts and interference she could make out Ken Barlow. The colour came and went, so mostly she watched in black-and-white. Jackie howled, teething. Darren arrived when it was dark. She could hear his voice out in the street shouting and laughing the way he does at the other lads, his mates in the Army. An engine roared, got angry, moved away. She heard Darren's anxious little pawing at the door. She opened it, Jackie in her arms and he was all kissing them both. She backed into the hall, they said ordinary things. She steadied herself, nervous.

She had Jackie twisting still in her arms when Darren came and kissed her again a long time this time leaning down to her as she carried, leaning back, the sack-weight of Jackie, always on the same cheek for a long one, moving all the time she smelled his soldiery uniformy smell and sweat and the leather smell of his boots well-shined. He took Jackie from her and the child mewed and pawed him. He played with his daughter like any man, wuzzle-wuzzle, nuzzling her fat belly, making her giggle no teeth coming yet but on the way, a sound that made the house safe.

Darren looked like a child, a wee baby, his fuzz not a proper moustache yet at all. When he put Jackie down he seemed to unloosen a greater weight than what she weighed, a little bundle of fun, God love her. Darren seemed to not know himself for a moment and he was looking around a lot, what's he looking for, it's his new home, ours. Holding Jackie up to high to the ceiling and he'd been all smiles but not now all of a sudden like when you remember something you wish you'd forget. She made him tea but he'd brought beer.

He click-popped a tin open and drank loudly, gulping. He sat down on one of the erratically-placed armchairs. He wasn't hungry, he'd eaten in the barracks, he told her this while he opened his uniform collar and slipped off his big black boots. He looked around the room; what do you think? He smiled, smiled. 'Now we're all moved in,' he said and smiled around and around, looking at the unpainted unpapered walls, at the open window.

She could see he was happy to be here, better than the flat and so long it took to get the Corporation to move them with the child and all.

'I should have been here,' he said, 'but you know I was working. I should have helped you shift things and move in.'

'I managed and now it's done,' she told him. Her finality, maybe confidence too, unsettled him. He turned away from her, cradling his beer, a big baby man in a funny outfit all greeny-brown. She felt enormous, big in the head and heart.

The TV was too loud, he turned down the sound of Questions & Answers, though he appeared to be, open-legged, staring at it. The room, the house, was getting colder. She turned on all the rings on the electric cooker and a stodgy heat filled the place, uncomfortable, airless. Darren told her he'd go out for fire in a minute but he had something to tell her first, so sit down.

She took up Jackie so's she wouldn't ramble off just like that, the size of her and all that energy to burn. Were we all like that? Darren switched the TV off. The silence was horrible, ice-cold like a chilly beer in your throat. She lit a cigarette. 'I'll have one, might as well,' said Darren. 'I don't like smoking in front of her.' 'Well,' she said, and said nothing.

He told her he'd been called up for Bosnia. Or Serbia. One of them. Jugoslavia anyway.

'Probably Bosnia,' she said for no reason in the wide world, she knew nothing about politics but she'd watched the news on TV a couple of times and knew the Army sent men out there and what happened. Now into her head came a tune she'd heard years ago by ABBA.

'Well,' said Darren, and his voice might as well have come out of the television for all she knew: 'I don't know. Maybe I'm not even supposed to say where.'

'When are you off?'

Jackie squealed under her feet, she'd put her down again, the weight of the babóg with her big creamy plucks and hardly a hair on her head, her Dad and Mam both agreed she looked the spit of Darren. The man upstairs in the flats had written a poem for her about Jackie when she was born and framed it and that was nice of him but where'd she put it?

Darren was not enjoying his cigarette, he slurped his beer to drown the smoke, he coughed anyway.

'Will I see if I can run a bath for you with hot water?' she said, remembering that now, now in this empty new house she had a comfortable bathroom and hot water all the time if she wanted it, all she'd to do was press a switch and when the red light came on the water was heating up automatically.

'Have you the recorder on?'

'It's not tuned,' she told him. And there'd be nothing worth recording anyway with the reception the way it was but maybe he could go out and get a film?

But Darren seemed, suddenly, to be made of cardboard, like a big cardboard soldier advertising a war movie outside the cinema when there was one on. She could see how he swam in a fragile kettle of greyish light, like a ghost might. Ghost stories of old houses in the dark alone. The sky outside and through the open window – which she'd better remember to close before they went to bed, you never knew what was out there her Dad had warned her – had turned a sour milky white and the orange lights of the city played up against it. It would be easy to be afraid out here if you let yourself.

'My Mam always told me never marry a soldier,' she said. She waited for Darren to laugh but he didn't, old joke.

'Well, you're moved in here and it's way better than the flat,' he said. 'Better for Jackie, too.'

There seemed to be no point at which their thoughts or words could touch. They both seemed to be talking to two other people, people who were not there but were there at the same time, suddenly as insubstantial as shadows on a wall.

She told him they were the only people moved into the estate, the very first. She told him about the woman and her arrogance and her husband on the docks. But Darren was far away. It was like you are when you have an argument and are not just ready for making up, the strange heat in the air between you.

'We should think about getting married when I get back.'

'Well, you know I'm ready for it if you are,' she said. She had the distinct feeling she'd said this before and he'd said what he'd said before.

'Now we've a decent place to live and all,' Darren said. Farther away and farther he sailed off through the blue darkening room. 'I'm away in two weeks. Me and the lads, you know them, you've met them out with me.'

'These are the lads you used to go out with and cancel meeting me for,' she said. The room pushed in on top of her. She smiled in the dark, she wondered if he could see her smiling, the memory of a light little thing like that but she'd cried then, and what they'd argued about before Jackie came along, she'd felt so neglected and he had his soldier mates after all.

'Now, it wasn't like that,' Darren said. 'You know.'

'You look after yourself, wherever they send you,' she said, when they'd had another little necessary silence.

'You can't kill a bad thing,' Darren said. He was talking, it was as if, to the blind TV set.

'I'm going to start a photograph album,' she said. 'When you're away. We've taken millions of photographs and they're all over the place, God knows where.'

Darren stood up. Shadow on his crotch. Army trousers, all pockets and baggy. He looked into the wall, the grey undecorated plaster. Will you miss me? he asked her. She couldn't tell if he was joking, Darren was never soppy.

'Of course I will,' she said. She would feel alone and weak for a while and she'd go to Mam's or her own parents almost every day or they'd come for her, she would be swallowed up, she would be back in the womb of them all. She said what she knew reassured him.

But thinking about him not there, not even a few miles away in the big stone-gated ugly barracks where at least if you went mad you could go and see him for two minutes made her feel a bit sick, like when you're going to faint but you don't.

'You'll not go off with some fancyman when my back's turned?'

She felt, but she couldn't see, his face in the flicking dark, the scared little boy's twitch in his voice. Not jealousy, Darren would never be jealous, he never cared what she did really, he was not possessive and thank God she'd heard of girls beaten for looking at a bloke. She grabbed Jackie up again in her arms, the suspicious hot waft of the child, was she filthy again? She saw Darren in the dark or the shape of him which is not the same.

'Soon as you're in that lorry I'll be out clubbing.'

Now this didn't mean anything good nor bad but it was what they said and was necessary for saying, you know anyway the way men are, some men anyway, soldiers or no soldiers. Like kids. She wouldn't do the dirt on him lonely and all as she'd be now and then anyway and she knew from the other girls that in any case when you brought a man back for a quick whatever-it-was and he heard the nipper squalling in the next room it put him off his stroke, off like a rocket, bye-bye. Thought you meant to trap him.

85

Cruel, some of the girls were, about men and the world. Just because bad things had happened to them.

She was building herself up with daft thoughts about maybe just once someone she fancied, but you wouldn't bring him back here where Darren was everywhere, in the walls and all. Or Jackie'd see. But she wasn't, deep down anyway, that type of girl. A kiss and cuddle was nothing and meant nothing, killed the night. Nothing else, definitely. Darren the only one. Whether he was here or not. But, then again, he'd never been away before. Even though the girls all said he would be from the start, being a soldier.

'You think of some awful things,' she told him now, scolded him. She touched his shoulder, the rough army cloth, the smell of his beery breath. She thought again about the poem in its frame for Jackie, where it was.

'Well, it's just like when we all heard this morning, it was a bit of a shock,' Darren said. 'The lads, like. Out of the blue.'

'I'm going to start a garden,' she said. 'I've never had a garden in my life and now I'm going to go mad out there, think of what it'll look like. I've always wanted a man to pick me up and take me to a house with a garden.'

'Cinderella or somebody,' Darren said. 'You're just a girl who never grew up.'

She saw Darren's face turn in the dark, turn slowly

like it was on rollers and carved out of stone, turn towards where a few stars had made their way through the pink yellow clouds in the high distance. The tin can in his hand was like something he was about to throw through the window but it was double-glazed and nothing was made of real glass anymore.

'They massacre whole villages and put them in deep holes,' Darren said. 'It's worse than the North.' Darren laying down a hard masculine emphasis on the three-syllabled word, massacre, a word that seemed to crack and fade at the end.

'But you won't be near any of them,' she said. She looked at his profile, black like you'd cut out of black paper in school. 'We're a neutral country. You're just there to keep the peace.'

Darren shrugged; a small distant mountain, a cliff, trembling in the dark. Doesn't matter, the certain horror and his own fear, she couldn't understand. For the lads to talk about, nervous cracking jokes, some of them never away from home, not far anyway.

Silence swept around them both like dust, like when you opened a door and dust and dry earth came in. She felt it fill her eyes. Darren's head, a roundy black bubble in the shadowy room, like an ornament or funny cuddly cushion bought as a present, what people think you like.

The sky broke apart and more stars fell through. It was hot and uncomfortable in the rooms now. She went out and turned off the cooker. She leaned over and closed the window, turned its funny-feeling lock. She closed the world out and the three of them in. Darren turned around and said with a breath that he wished they had candles, a bare electric light-bulb which was what they had hanging from the ceiling until she went out and bought a few shades wasn't very nice.

There were things you could do with a house like this, he said. Beats the flat, Jesus. He seemed to be talking to someone else in the room she couldn't see. Someone who understood him better than she did. The heat in the rooms bowed slightly and withdrew. She'd put up curtains, get them cheap, Darren's Mam was good at doing things like curtains.

'I must buy some incense too,' she said.

The smell of it, nice. Places far away, not here. Travel brochure places where people wrote poetry, like the bloke on the top flat. Sun on balconies and the air a salty blue.

Where Darren would be the sun might shine all the time, or it might rain and be awful. She imagined scenes from a movie they'd watched where savage hordes launched themselves out of black forests. No language that anyone could understand, or maybe they'd all speak like the girl in the petrol station where you could go late at night for milk and cigarettes who spoke English but too loudly, as if she wanted her sentences to carry all the way home, wherever that was. A girl who looked like a model from the kind of glossy magazine you always found in a doctor's waiting room.

She saw Darren in the dark, a mere silhouette, not really Darren but the ghost of Darren. Something shivered just below her heart. She thought to herself, I don't want to make love to him tonight and I don't even know why.

She imagined cold dark light, painted in it all of them, looking like corpses in dust. Jackie should be in her bed, she'd make up the cot in the same room as she'd sleep with Darren and not wake her. Darren leaned over suddenly and switched the TV back on. Silver light exploded in the room.

There would be so little to do and so much space to do it in, with him gone. But even with him here, sitting near her, he was gone. She felt that if she were to reach for him he would disappear. With an even deeper shiver she realised how insubstantial they both were, how the baby was real but they had perhaps stopped being flesh and blood things and were now little shells of bone and skin filled with shadows. You could only really see them in blinding light.

Darren would keep the peace. He and his mates, their little stashes of porn magazines and cheap beer. The hordes would wait, wait in the black trees and when the time was right they would come out of their

89

hiding places with horns on their heads screaming and licking new blood. And back in these new rooms she'd stalk the stifling silence while the baby cried and soiled herself and no map in the world would bring her closer to a place of safety. We're so fragile, she thought, so made of nothing, really.

She stood up so quickly that she made Darren turn his head to watch her as she walked out of the glaring room, and she felt the blast of cold noisy light on her back, her shadow imprinted on the wall in front of her; a quivering image, black on white.

# Ship of Fools

'He last on this savage promontory shored
 His logical weapon...'

Richard Murphy: *Wittgenstein and the Birds*

The boat groaned in on a high tide.

Rusting in the masts and sides, some sort of name painted over on the stern, it appeared lashed to our stone quay like an old sea story. From the start, no one wanted it there; it stank almost visibly.

He put it about that he was a refugee from something hideous in darker middle Europe. There was a romantic touch of the gypsy on him. He said he had been a painter. Often in the following days he was to be seen painting something, God knows where he came by the materials. He would sit by the quayside and paint their hideous boat. When the tide went out the vessel leaned precariously against the quay wall, a tired old rogue of a thing, a hulking embarrassment.

The rest of them appeared in and out the local pubs, following fiddlers and singers and tapping the sides of their beer glasses with combs and other objects, putting on some show of being primal and in contact with the music of the earth, I suppose. I've been working in the Life Assist Centre for long enough and I've seen this sort of thing before. They come in, dubious Cockneys, they look for advice on how to mend their lives, not really wanting it, I suspect. I point them in the direction of the dole. Everyone's happy.

The Life Assist Centre is a neglected place, dragged down by the weight of hopelessness shoved into its insatiable mouth every open day. I dress casual, you're supposed to. Nothing officey, nothing intimidating. But it's myself who feels intimidated. On the walls there are displayed all the hopeless under-classy posters of a new world if you'll only sign this, ask about that. In truth there is no saving a whole swathe of people. There are things you cannot say openly and that's one of them.

So when he came in, smiling that appalling, uncomprehending smile, I smiled back as I'm supposed to and prepared myself for the usual helpful rituals. He was young enough under the earthy untidiness. He wore the sort of brown tweedy jacket that much older men, farmers, perhaps, wear to tend cattle and do other messy jobs. His white shirt collar was filthy, his hair short, black and greasy. You look at people like that and say There but for the Grace...It's difficult not to despise them.

'I can teach to paint.'

'Your name is?'

'Painting. I can do.'

He made birdy shapes in the air, or so I interpreted the fine, almost delicate wavings of his long pianist's paint-stained fingers. They'd been around for a week, near enough, with their dreadful boat. What, I wondered, were the three or four others, a long-skirted, barefoot girl among them, doing while he was mouthing in front of me?

'I must have your name.'

I'd produced a form to hide behind. Over his shoulder in the sloping empty street a sunlight of sorts quivered and slopped against the grey pavements. The village had a writers' group and amateurish workshops on print-making, pottery, even Tarot-card reading. Blow-ins like myself, some of them retired from the world, others just young and strangely sad, ran most of them. Perhaps he'd be lucky.

His name was unpronounceable, of course. He spelled it for me, coming close, his breath unhealthy and hot and thick on my face. His clothes smelled of cigarettes and stale beer and sweat. I wrote it down. Was it like this for bored officials at Ellis Island? This making and remaking of language? Conjuring up identities?

I scribbled, guessing him into comprehensible existence. I showed him what I'd written. He frowned,

93

then perhaps thought not to unbalance things. He nodded vigorously. We went through a similar ritual over his age. Place of birth?

His story bore the strained rhythm of a recitation, a poem at a reading, intonations here and there for effect; a story whose truth was hidden under too many applied coats of panic and loss. The more he acted, the more I knew he was describing truth as a kaleidescope of probabilities. It was an odd moment or two. Perhaps he had learned that the truth without gestures only weighs half as much. Or perhaps it was the weak sun brightening the street over his shoulder and the mood I was in.

I mentioned his painting. Animated again, this time all movement funnelled through his round brown eyes, he spoke of a city the vowels of whose name I barely caught, a university. There was tragedy of a sort in the story, foreign and alien tragedy, all the more romantic and unreal for its cargo of distance and exotic place-names. He chanted a litany of mistakes, misfortunes, bad luck and murder. It all had the quick development of a novel. Somehow he'd escaped in the end, but from what was never quite defined. In any case, he'd met his odd friends the boat people and landed here, a bare village by the wide ocean with a broken castle and new bungalows painted pink for the new young rich from elsewhere; foreigners, so far as the locals were concerned, like himself. He held out his hands, palms upwards, and leaned his head to one side. I hated him for the cliché he made of himself.

'I teacher of paint at home. I speak English. Some people come, no money. Find job to do. Go away. Not trust.'

'You mean some people use us because we're a bit thick,' I said.

'Yes,' he replied, blinking. 'They use.'

But he wasn't one of them, no. He tried to make that clear. He was a good man, he said. As a token of this, he said suddenly:

'People tell you big family so you give money. I have no family, I work only for me. Is better?'

Mischievously, I held my tongue, resisted the urge to tell him it didn't matter, that he'd never be anything but an outsider and under suspicion here. Let him learn for himself. I'd even seduced some local women to gain acceptance, but it hadn't worked, I broke no silence when I entered a pub. And they were the sorts of women who giggled in the pubs afterwards and had known one another since schooldays. They were going nowhere, there was no need for them ever to grow up. Schoolgirls they'd be still, at sixty. Through them, I frustrated myself the more.

A brief slither of resentment caressed my abdomen like an unwanted hand. My life was a small round thing, rolled up and down that sloping street behind this immigrant's back. He showed me papers, complex things with green harps on them. I ignored them. Suddenly I was irritated.

'Write a notice,' I told him, my voice raised for no reason. I pointed to the wall, to the mean window: 'I'll put it up for you on the wall. There. An advertisement. Don't forget to hand it to me.'

I spoke slowly, as you would to a child.

Of course, he must hand it to me. I would be the one to physically tack it to the wall, tape it on the window; you had to make some show of authority. Couldn't have him thinking he had a right to do it himself.

'Yes,' he nodded, obviously relieved. 'Thank you, yes.'

He backed out of the front door. Over his head, dangling from the wall, flapped a flightless poster of a pregnant teenager and the words Scared? Lonely?

Evening threw marvellous sky-colours over the prim, settled harbour. Small rowing boats jiggled here and there, from bigger yachts there came the fairy belling of metal clamps, rings, a thousand other bits and pieces, and a triangle of swans cleaved the blue dark water off the stony, wrack-black shore. There were clouds over the far islands, brewing up out of the western ocean. A breeze ran before them. The odour of salt, brine, ammonia hung in the air like smoke; a dog scampered on a thin stretch of trimmed grass, pissing from ancient stone bollard to bollard. The great dead stone warehouse, windows shut like the eyes of the dead, faced the bracing new sea wind and the coming smack of rain, stared eyeless over the rolling masts and the ropes and the furring sea and the rusty, ugly bulk of the vessel upon which my client had arrived.

This, then, was my nightly walk home. I took it all in, its utter, even sunny loneliness, its village terror like a child's fear of the dark muttering under everything. Scraps of old rumour hung from the trees, crows gossiped on the rooftops. Or round the ceiling of my skull, at least.

A heaviness fell with the drop of the working day. In the pitiful office I had at least a sense of purpose and of myself. Alone, walking where eager tourists took photographs and pointed camcorders and said aloud how lovely everything was, I felt a cold sadness like a small death flowering in me. I went in to The Gravel Walks.

There was a photograph on a mock-stone wall of what the pub had been like twenty years ago, a small thatched place with black-capped, crow-like men outside it. A whole field had been swallowed up by the new place, a green-painted two-storey building with mock-wooden pillars and plastic lifebelts, lobsters and even plastic nets, prefabricated, a sort of big child's kit, splattered everywhere inside. A fake ancient map showed where a slice of island had been born out of the Great Portuguese Earthquake. The music from the bat-like speakers on the walls was bumpa-bumpa-bumpa trash of the sort kids do drugs to and die by.

Over the mirror behind the glistening, whitewood bar hung proudly a photograph of the proprietor with his arm around the shoulders of a recently disgraced politician. There was a piano in one corner of the room and the room was mushroomed with small round tables and stools. The TV was always on, even with the music from the speakers, even when a few local musicians played their jigs and reels in the corner at weekends.

A couple of elderly locals in caps turned to look at me as I came in. There was no hint of friendliness. The white-shirted barman kept his head down and polished glasses fussily, talking into the floor. Every now and then one of his customers would nod. I grabbed a rattled copy of the Daily Mirror, glanced at pregnant superstars and read a couple of paragraphs on two schoolboys accused of decapitating a neighbour's cat. Over whiskey and water and a toasted cheese sandwich, its cellophane wrapping melted into the bread, I stared over the long barren field of evening.

Towards closing-time a healthy argument about music, politics and Gaelic football, about which I knew nothing, had eased a gathering isolation.

It was, I suspected, an isolation felt by all of us, the stalwart half-dozen, who perched and swivelled on our bar stools like exotic yapping birds. Someone mentioned the hulking boat in the harbour, the filth of it and of its long-haired crew. And that foreigner, that Pole, or Russian, or whatever he was. Jesus! The village was a refugee camp!

I despised these bitter, destroyed half-farmers, half-fishermen, glistening with the beery sweat of their various lonely dooms. Yet I nodded as if something controlled me, something outside myself pulled the strings. I went home with back-slappings and the smack of chilled, white salted air in the face. I abhor injustice. I made coffee, put some paper in the ancient Oliver typewriter, wrote a letter to a local newspaper. It doesn't matter what I wrote about. The pressure of my fingers on the old keys was reassuring at first, then exciting. There was power here in what I was doing. I was reaching out in to the world. I felt filled with something weighted and dark when I'd finished. I read over my letter. I found an envelope, a stamp, posted the letter at the end of a long, silent walk along the quays to the Post Office slot in the wall. Then I walked back again, meeting no one, drenched in the salty darkness, ears full of the sing-song tinkle of the rocking boats.

I saw him once or twice over the coming weeks, the painter. He smiled broadly at me, as if he were a schoolboy under surveillance. Look how well I'm doing. The seeming despair in all of this was too much for me to look at. I hated seeing him, dreaded that he would ever come over to me, say anything. By this time he had acquired a couple of teenage students and they huddled in front of the harbour on good weather days with their sketch pads and even their rudimentary watercolour sets or important-looking tins of paint, children enjoying themselves, feeling themselves to be different.

The others from the boat haunted the pubs where listless, half-hearted jigs and reels were played, and they joined in the dreary ballads of young men dying for Ireland's freedom, miming the words. By this, I suppose, they imagined it was possible to blend in to the village, or some aspect of it. I knew better. Acceptance here was not a song you could sing or imitate. No outsider knew the music of this village.

When the weather blew up, the painter would adjourn his classes. His pupils, clutching round him for a brief moment out of courtesy, would then disperse. When he was accused, under the breath, of inviting the teenagers on to the rusting vessel, I knew it was a lie. So did the bar-stool retailer of the libel. But it didn't matter.

Arguments, raised voices, were now common in the smokey, brown-aired music pubs. One of the painter's boat companions would attempt a song, something daftly Irish such as Carrickfergus. At once an ancient huddle at the bar would turn drunkenly, mutter unintelligibly but loudly. Interrupted, the singer would ask for quiet; worse, he would ask, in that mock-Cockney which by now irritated us all, for respect. I would stand by a door, glass in hand, my mouth leprous with nicotine and take a brazen delight in the young man's helplessness. Someone had remarked that he'd seen a letter of mine in the paper; he could not recall its subject. But this conferred upon me a certain status. So I smiled with the rest as the hated youth, his song dead, twisted a rat's tail of hair in his dirty-nailed fingers and stared around the room. Some local girls, too young to be served in a public bar but getting drunk there anyway, eyed up the strangers. Further proof, of course, of their inherent evil. In shops, fat middle-aged women, all trace of femininity erased, worn down, would speak in harsh men's voices about castrating anyone who made a daughter of theirs pregnant.

I'd been long enough in the village to know this would happen anyway; I had my brace of single mothers, children themselves, red-eyed, harassed, struggling to maneouvre the push-chairs over the single step, troop into the Life Assist Centre before the hell-ship had docked.

I could feel the air thicken over the village, giving us something new and thrilling to breathe. Not the salt of the sea now but the salt of blood, an invigorating, lusty tang, almost sexual. The weather changed and stayed, hot and starry in its daily turn. In the Centre I stripped down to my shirt and rolled up the sleeves. I felt rakish and younger. The painter came in, wide-faced with fear and agitation.

'My paints, brushes,' he stuttered. His hands flew like scared birds.

'What about them?'

It was a beautiful day. He was a speck in the day's clear eye.

'They have been robbed of me! I have nothing.'

I felt the weight of his nothing. It was a particular thing, it had a certain unforgettable taste, I'd sipped it once or twice. I did not want intimations of this nothingness pleading with me to be recognised. His brown, Gypsy face fascinated me in its agitation. His flying ringless hands were now the brown leaves of a tree dancing at the end of the thin branches of his arms. He was a tree, black against the sun of the sloped street outside, interfering with the passage of the good white light.

'Talk to the police, then.'

They would take no notice, of course. But he knew this from God only knew what number of previous lives.

He shook his head, assumed a solemn expression. Absurdly I recalled the barman's ignorant habit of addressing you while staring at the floor. The world was full of simple ignorance.

'I don't understand how you think I can help you, then. This is the wrong place.'

The last phrase slipped out and I heard it even before I spoke it. Yes, this was indeed the wrong place, for both of us. Something mischievous or even malign had thrown us into this village, searching for better things, a life, love, whatever. We'd run aground on the arid shores of village life. The village spoke about me behind my back as surely as they spoke of him behind his.

But I resented him the more for knowing this. No one had the right to consider him my equal in any sense. No one had the right to judge us on the same terms. He was a fucking foreigner, for God's sake. Christ, he looked like a tinker!

My outrage, his dwindling complaint, met in the stale hot cigaretty air of the single room of the Centre.

And I noticed his smell. Or perhaps it was my own.

I opened my arms and hands in a pontiff-like gesture.

'I'm afraid we can't supply money for things like paint and brushes, if that's what you want.'

This was not strictly true. But I had no intention of going through elaborate procedures with him or indicating other services which might help him. I felt the power, the drunkenness, of having him at my mercy. Behind him, a shadow flew down the sloping street, then the sun whitewashed everything. I had an image of how nice it would be to tramp up over the mountains on a day like this, the breeze blushing your face, the sea below you all the way to America.

The door behind him opened and an old man came in. The painter turned, saw the old man, gave a slight bow and left without another word.

Not long after that the grafitti appeared. Scrawled along the side of the boat nudging the quay, the grand, righteous word pervarts. With an 'a'. It went with the utterly unfounded rumour that the painter was taking local children on board the boat. You heard this sort of thing in the Gents in The Gravel Walks. The stink of urine smoked the words into your nostrils, burned them there.

Tourists arrived, buses bigger than the world, purring outside our ruins while dangerously fat people in whites and yellows and oranges and blues and even stripes drank Guinness and photographed each other drinking Guinness. They crawled over our ancient castle like gaudy ants. The sun glossed the small waves of the harbour, the water turned a Pacific blue. The sunsets were red and mottle-skied. Schoolgirls smoked illicit cigarettes under the awning of the rusting, piss-smelling bus shelter and eyed the French teenagers, the small Japanese adolescents with their forever smiles and e-cameras, the Yank guys, gawky and dangerously innocent, with their peaked caps on backwards.

The world came to the village, polishing it up. Musicians came from all over the county to play in the pubs, too-fast jigs and reels, hopelessly bad Country 'n' Irish. Tourists tried to sing Irish songs under the pale eye of hand-held video cameras. There was money going round, there were rivers of piss in the early morning streets, yellowish vomit hardening in the morning sunlight on the pavements. Empty cigarette-packets and used condoms married in the gutters. The sound of glass breaking mixed with loud laughter and the hysterical, whining woman's screel of bows across fiddle-strings. The midday Mass every Sunday was in Irish, which the Catholic American tourists loved. It reminded him of the days of Latin, one of them told me; what you can't understand stays magical.

The painter had obtained, as if by a dark magic of his own, more paints, brushes, and he sat sketching and painting down by the quayside every morning and for an hour or two after lunch, eating soup and bread rolls and drinking black coffee in The Gravel Walks. No one made any remarks about him. It wouldn't have done to have upset the munching and drinking tourists sitting around and about. Some perverse and mercenary reasoning had set him up there, unwitting, as a living advertisement for the cultural diversity of the village. Look at us, the village seemed to say through him; look how colourful and rich is our understanding of the world.

His companions from the boat gathered around him on the quayside, sipping from tins of cider or smoking joints. The rich aroma of hashish drifted over the stones and the sea and the tourists turned up their noises and frowned. But he sold a painting here and there. The others, I'd no doubt, lived off him. He smiled a lot. Perhaps in some men that's a sign of their knowledge of impending disaster. The music rattled and screeched like bad brakes out of every pub door, the grunting and drunken heaving and bucking against the old brick walls gasped on.

In the wee hours of one of these amazed mornings, fire broke out on the boat. The painter and two others, asleep, were trapped and suffocated. The fire licked upwards through the messy rigging; I can imagine stars of fire burning into the wide open black heavens. It was muttered that the painter's body had been found with the hands outstretched, claws of hands. Men and women hungry for horror said things like this. There was also an element of the exotic and thrilling in the notion of fire twisting the stranger's body into something unimaginably un-human. Certainly I hoped that he hadn't woken up, that his paints and thinners had burned him quickly. I had obsessional spurts of grotesque images, his mouth crisped back off his teeth, his tongue black, swollen, that idiot smile of his etched into his skull with fire. Perhaps I had the ugliness in my head already and I needed it to have a face, something vaguely human.

The fat red growling fire engines on the quay brought out the tourists' cameras. Then there were the police, striding big men in civvies who drove flash cars with city polish on their dark sleek metal; men who ignored the local Guards, who had, it seemed, nothing in common with them. The ambulances took the bodies away, covered stretchers moving in grey speed from the cordoned-off blackened boat to the white immaculateness of the bright lights of their silver and white interiors. Such a miracle of movement on the village quay that day.

The deaths quietened us for a time. A Mass was said to a packed church. Flowers came out of nowehere, crinkling cellophaned bunches laid on the altar rails. Meanwhile, the bodies were in a mortuary somewhere. The Mass, I sensed, was not so much about the strange dead but about ourselves, we who had been there before them; it was an exorcism of sorts. If there was guilt, the Mass removed it; we smoked outside on the steps, annoyed that the service had taken so long, the weather fine and cool, the trees fat with black birds and their high nests, every wrinkle in the plump distant mountains visible and distinct. There was an unspoken agreement, like a virus carried in the air, that no one had an opinion to share about the cause of the fire.

Days follow days and he stays with me. My roomy clutter contains one of his paintings, gaudy unnatural colours but bright, bright. No one knows I purchased one from him, a view of our ruined castle with the sea splashed in black blue all around it. Nothing moves in the picture, neither human being nor flying bird. Even the water is frozen.

I remember him, I see him painting on the quay and I see him pleading in front of me at the Centre. How little I know of him beyond these images. He is a cypher, a ghost, moving in and out of himself, in and out of the mind of the village I have made, or tried to make, my own. The sloping main street and the old grey stones and salt-rotted red brick of disused buildings contain him, or that part of him which rises upwards and curls itself into local myth.

National newspapers have sent their perfumed columnists and small town Irish life has been called many things. Suddenly the village is older, blacker, more dangerous. The Famine graveyard on the top of the hill is haunted by journalists trying to get background, a feel for place.

The police investigation is still going on, they're never far away, obvious in their ordinary clothes, sipping drinks, watching, listening. They are civil and will strike up a conversation with you as good as any one. But they are listening with their voice, you can see that.

Men whose lives are dead leaves on a pond, dried up inside from lack of women or mother loss or God knows what, mutter drunkenly about how no good could possibly follow people like that, the outsiders.

The word outsider has taken on a different

resonance, significance, than foreigner. Language is shifting, sprouting new fruit, day to day as the deaths by fire on the boat become more real.

I do not know what to think about the fire that killed him. I remember him and his smile and how I enjoyed him being lower in the village social scale than myself and that is all. I enjoy my guilt, live off it. I've been drawn closer to the village by my having been here when he died. There was something, I suppose, absurdly sacred about what happened to him. Those others of his companions drifted away, the not unattractive girl with them; the boat hulks still, rust the colour of blood, blackening, no gulls will settle on any part of her.

As our language alters in the very air around me, as people greet me every day in the street and stop and discuss the weather, cows calving, someone building a currach, his face takes on an iconic glow in my memory. Now they call me the writer because of all those letters of mine that appear in newspapers.

But I do not know who to defend next. A new world slinks forward, drooling. Lawyers send warning letters to newspapers. Writers sue one another. The world is heavier than it has ever been. The poets are dead or dying. Nothing is true. We are warned, we are warned; the rooms in which we try to breathe begin to shrink.

Yet we must be involved.

(Gilford, Co Armagh – for John Arden and Margaretta D'Arcy)

# Bolus Ground

'There are hundreds of other gifts of painting which
are not at all involved with moral conditions...'

John Ruskin: *The Unity of Art*

There is music in the way water bubbles in gutters and
drains. The sort of music one finds in paintings,
sometimes. Not paintings of musical instruments, not
like that. Something natural and fixed. I don't need to
explain, you know what I mean.

It was raining heavily, my pork-pie hat, my
trademark to some, was sopping. Little globules of
silver water had formed their own universes on the
fabric. I'm a familiar figure. The odd wave here and
there. The club-foot is what they see first, or rather,
my up-down hobble. The cane's for show.

There's been a lot of unnecessary, in my view, fuss,
about this Bacon business. I knew him. Spent hours
pissed in that refuse tip mews kip; squatting, leaning,
hardly ever sitting, nothing to sit on. Brushes in butter
bean tins, my tripping over his enormous VAT 69

111

carton while he fondled his miniature David to illustrate some point or other. He was reading Nietzsche, and trying to teach himself German to read the original, which I thought was daft and said so: German for Adults. He'd filched from me a rather heavy tome on Velasquéz, whom some said he painted like, though I never could see it. I thought he'd leaned a bit much towards Picasso. The naked light bulb motif is out of Guerníca. Then again, some said his brutish father used to lock him in an unlighted broom-cupboard for days when he was a child. Who knows what light bulbs mean?

Sometimes we'd just sit and listen to his transistor radio. He liked music. Once he told me that all his paintings were about himself. The naked light bulb was about illuminating the horror of our lives, he said. The false, fake Apollo casting his limp light over a catastrophic world.

Some say my style apes his. I dispute that, though of late I've begun to concentrate even more on the human form. This new show, for instance, is about human form and what happens to it. Corruption, if you like.

The good days in London didn't last long, more's the pity. London, the Grail for some. And there was talk, a cottage in Cornwall, Goldsmith students. I think there was some idea of creating a second and decidedly half-arsed Camden Town Group, Lord help us, but there was too much drink and messing about. I ignored the gossip, let them get on with whatever they got on with. There were many crude attempts to discuss Francis' art back then. And mine, which wasn't as fiery or as mad. The head and sides of beef thing, though, had given some of them the opportunity to say he'd tied himself to outmoded notions about trauma and the last world war. Bollocks. His paintings are all about himself, even when they're not.

I don't think he was fair to those who loved him. I think he hated himself for this but was unable to do anything about it. Hence the self-rage in his work. But if you want to hear any more about him and those days, read my memoirs.

I crossed this bridge once and asked a begging child if I could draw him. He asked me for money. I told him to piss off. He knocked the spontaneity out of it, for me. Cheapened the business.

I remember when underneath the Guinness barges blew thick brown smoke up into your face and the air was full over the river and of the homely smell of hops. Things have changed. I've changed. Can't chase anymore, can't run after anything or anyone. When that dies out of life, life implodes, like they say a TV set does. I long for the days, not always but now and then, when everything we did was illegal. Added spice.

Now it's all young shaven-headed pretty boys dressed in black acting the artist for the columns of

Saturday newspapers. No life, no violence, left.

You have to have a nail in your soul, the heart snagging on a rusty wire, as my old friend, bless him, John Noble once said to me. John was a teacher, a good one, having done the decent thing and given up art when he couldn't do it well. I held his hand as cancer dissolved him. He didn't complain. He faded into the bedclothes and disappeared. It's a long time ago now. The room was full of the sweet smell of flesh decaying, I remember that.

My scarf, wrapped around my neck, has become saturated with rain. It feels like a snake trying to strangle me. The light is beginning to go, the sky is the colour of tinned salmon. I've often thought of plunging headfirst into the old Plurabella. Tell me the man who hasn't. Now I give the river a passing glance, as it were, a kind of side of the eye regard. It's often been a comfort to me that I could take my own life.

Now some say that this sort of melancholy has taken root in some of my pictures. I hate the word root, it reminds me of illness, things going deep down and killing. There is, let me be clear, no room for sentiment in painting. At least not any more. The age of sentiment is long passed. Perhaps it ended after the Great War, who knows, and I could drag up the names of painters, but I'm not going to bother. What I paint now is the most unsentimental subject you could imagine: the revenge of life on the body, the way we decay, all stops out, all systems go, over to the worm. In a way that's what Francis painted; the gape-mouthed dissolution of the body and the soul. Under a naked light-bulb. Everything liquifying. Nothing solid, nothing certain. He took out a plastic lighter once, a green one, and held the flame up to my face. He could be frightening. In a loving sort of way.

No, I was never a lover there, not me. Perhaps could have been, I was a drunken Irishman like himself and he liked pissed Paddys. I remember a certain leprechaunish playwright whom I met, starkers, in that kip of a flat. Sings shtum, nowadays. Someone else mentions this in a book. I think he could fall in love but a painterly insanity made him break the love up into bits he could paint with. I'm only mentioning my preferences, as they're called, because they're old news anyway.

I'm walking now towards my doom. I'm always nervous at an opening. People have come to expect a certain darkness about my work and I sincerely hope they'll not be disappointed. But there's something extra in these works. The Table IV might make someone throw up, but that's all right as long as nobody compares me to lovely Francis.

Traffic at this time of day. No manners. There's a rush on this city that's not good for its heart. I hobble clubbily between cars and feel the heat come off the engines and out of the eyes of their drivers. I feel like a target. I've never driven, just as well, maybe. Terry offered to have someone pick me up, and I should've taken the offer, but that's me. What I'm worried about right now, even as I see the yellow square of light from the big front window of the gallery reflecting, doing marvellous colour work, on the wet street, is to have some decent press. Critics I loathe.

One in particular, and he's here, naturally.

I open the glass door, a drenched Claudius, remove my porky. The beetle-black tailored back of a decent critic shifts itself and he offers me his hand. More hands materialise, it becomes a Beckett play. The noise is conversation and music from the walls: Allighiero's Artemis Concerto, First Movement, followed by Lotti's Crucifixus and then Gesualdo's Tenebrae factae sunt. All looped, as I've asked, the lighter Allighiero blending subtly with the darker others. There's canapés and white and red plonk and pinky things on sticks. Redfaced men in various degrees of sweat smile and kiss the cheeks of women of a certain age who smell, as I squeeze past them, of talc and the process of drying out. Or is it up? All this is not for the young. Old age is not for the young, is it? Well, then. Neither are the painterly rantings...

My hand shoots out like a predatory bird.

'Harry. Good of you to come.'

Harry resembles something by Beatrix Potter. His fat shape is cast in a Plaster-of-Paris-toned suit which clings to the fat folds of his legs and arms. He has charcoal eyes and a lizard's mouth, always wet and red. Harry emerged from some hatchery in the Yank mid-west, did no good in a nameless university, ended up here and whipped onto a newspaper as a critic before the ink's dry on his passport-stamp. As if the Yank drawl is what post-revolutionary Ireland respects in place of Oxbridge. You loathe Harry because he knows nothing about art and gets paid to ladle this nothing back out to you. A dangerous nothing, let me add, because it's a black and dark negative that can do damage. You may suspect, from the anger in his reviews at times, that he didn't get on with his Dad. Or perhaps got on too well.

But it's my opening and I shake his hand wetly. He's cradling a gin and tonic. A soft-ground etching of a human being.

'Wouldn't like to wake up to one of those on my wall.'

'You won't, dear boy. I promise.'

I enjoy falling into the sad old queen routine for people like Harry. They expect it. It gives them a tale to tell.

'Bringing home the Bacon again?'

'Schoolboyish, Harry. Are we going to act the cunt tonight? Excuse me.'

I move through the sweat and talc. Give them what they want, John, bless him, used to say. Terry comes over. So thin. I think he was born sickly looking. Every time I shake his hand it's like saying goodbye. But he's the best. His thin grey face shatters into a smile of enthusiasm. His handshake is firm and he can look you straight in the eye.

'This is very good work.'

A camera flashed beside us.

'I hope I flog one or two.'

'Give me your hat. And the scarf. And the stick.'

'The stick's my prop, Terry.'

Sure enough, a red spot had appeared on a frame across the room. The only sort of red spots a painter wants to see – now who said that first?

Terry busies himself chatting people up. He's good at that. You have to allow for his abrupt comings and goings. It's the business end of things and it's very necessary. I, meanwhile, hoke through the catalogues. The reproductions are decent. The Gothic font is a bit over the top, but there you are: The Arrogance of Flesh. So, I turn and view my own work, try to stand outside it, as it were.

The Table IV is a set of five humanesque figures, redly disembowelled, emerging tortuously from a dark background or space, all on unprimed canvas. There's not much to be said about them beyond that, from my point of view. They never look quite so large hung as when they're snug on the easel. But they are attracting red spots, or perhaps growing them, for all I know.

Attitude is a tall work, virtually devoid of human shapes, but you can see them, as it were, bleeding into the bright foreground if you stand back a bit. Reclining Mask is a lovely macabre little thing, with two head-shapes, skulls more correctly, leering out, mouths open, from a dark background. Nasty young things in an alley? Scumble is used here, oils of course. I'm not a great acrylics fan, really. The scumble effect is to make the skulls almost go in and out of each other, and the glazing is very light. Resurrection V is one of a series I'm doing, and I thought it would do no harm to bring out a finished piece here. The body shape, armless, split, is doing a chiaroscuro stretching trip upwards, imitating religious painting of a certain type that calls itself visionary. Now the background is not shaded, but deeply blued and greened, suggesting growth and emptiness, using the optical mixtures routine, so that it's almost pointillism but not quite, though nothing much can be gained from the work by standing up close to it. The human figure is drawn first and I've left the drawn lines visible; they have become like whisps of smoke around the torso. I'm particularly happy with Christ Seized, a sort of yelling head dissolving behind bars. Bacon there, fair enough. But it's a homage. The flesh-tones fade, my handling...

'Ladies and Gentlemen, if we could have hush for one moment...'

Terry does the needful. Great MC. I'm squaring up

119

to a bulbous G and T and finding my form. Terry, frail as the skeleton of something lying a long time underground, addresses the audience and sings my praises. A factotum turns off Lotti. I respond with a self-effacing load of guff. It's what's expected. Then from nowhere appears an image of gentle John Noble, dying. I feel something swelling in my throat, seizing my voice. A cancer of loss?

'I'd like to remember a dear deceased friend in this show,' I say, 'A great teacher and artist in the real sense, John Noble. Thank you.'

Terry hear-hears. He knew John. Terry's wife came over to London when John was dying. John and I were not lovers, as some suggested, but we were friends from the Goldsmith days. He was the first artist I'd ever watch die, but not the last. I had thought we were immortal. Funny how the passing of years sometimes does not diminish things, but enhances them.

'Bravo,' Terry says, and pats me on the back. 'A lovely gesture. Is it his anniversary or something?'

'No, nothing like that.'

'Bravo. Well done.'

He moves away. I'm left, for a moment, with my thoughts, which have turned a nasty shade of grey. I feel old, suddenly. Well, hardly suddenly. But I feel what it means now, its weight. The passing of something irretrievable. An energy going out of you, more than physical. A coming to terms which is a refusal to come to terms. Perhaps it'll be quick, for me. Or slow, like John, silent, wordless, floating backwards and backwards until you fall off the earth with a sigh. You reach an age and you know you'll die. You don't know that at twenty. But at my age, you do. It's all you have left to look forward to, in some ways. The end of all this, whatever it is.

I can't remember sitting down, but I'm sitting down when old Harry drawls his way over. He stands over me fatly. I fake a grimace.

'Tell me you aren't just doing your Bacon thing here. I need to know. Really.'

'Is this a recent Americanism, Harry, to say "need" when you mean "want"?'

'What? Tell me.'

'There's nothing to tell. You see what you see, Harry. It's not up to me to guide you around my paintings.'

'I see Bacon, is what.'

'So you keep saying. Interminably. You risk becoming a bore.'

A woman's yelpish laugh cracks over the room. A snapper is scribbling names in his notepad. Terry is pouring wine. Drunkenness is taking over. The buying hunger is fading.

Harry won't go away, he's a tad unsober himself. His drawl is sheathing about my nerves like a disease. He draws closer. Intimacies, Christ? I can smell his

121

aftershave, see the red welt where his white shirt is digging into his fat neck. A shirtmaker's name; same place our better-class fake politicians go. It's all fake now, a voice in my head, probably John Noble's, tells me. Harry has taken up another gin and tonic and begun to sweat. I think of the last time I read his column, two brick-shaped lines of type under his grinning postage-stamp photograph. It reminded me of the images of the deceased under glass I'd seen in village graveyards in France, the South, land of the Cathars, the sky blue and the earth yellow and the vines grey and sturdy-looking. A Toulouse hotel in the old red-light district; a woman, too old, in fishnet stockings playing the Lotto with a Cognac in her hand. The great walled towns, the heat, the coffees in the open air; en plein air. Days painting life and light and colour and music down by the Garonne, in the reeds, naked sometimes. The slumbering heat. The train station at Toulouse with its iron raftering, its tracks running on and on so very lonely. I'd come back that summer to a Dublin grey and torturous, and the old crowd had asked me where I'd been, like mother hens. A photograph of Francis and John taken outside a bookshop in London that's now a bloody take-away. Round-faced Francis, slightly sad always, cravatted Sainted Francis-of-a-Cissy, as some adolescent giggly toilet-wag scrawled on the jacks of what pub was it? The rage in Spain, the illustrator whose work depicting

Lope de Vega in a whorehouse had caused Franco to ban him from ever working in Spain again. The rage, the anger, the holy violence of love-making. Lovers among the Arab boys in Paris. The rue de Rivoli in the heat, shimmering like a glaring shovel of concrete shoved into the furnace of the city. Too young, under the flowers and the sun, ever to think of death, ever to paint death of any kind or watch it paint over a loved life. Oh, I told them of the heat and wine and the gouts of energy and the paint-stained fingers scrawling over your wet back....

'Can you just, like, elaborate your obvious need...'

He'd made a move for his notebook. This was official Harry. I hated him, the sound and shape of him. Anger grew up in me and it had a salty taste. Had we painted our arses off to end up here under the Judgement of Harry? I'd actually bitten my tongue: was I taking fits now? Maddened, wounded, fed up, I shouted.

'I'll elaborate all over your face, you fat little pork-plumber. Do you know, dear Harry, that we used to fuck Yank sailors in London in the good old days just to keep our hand in, so to speak?'

Knew I shouldn't have said it, of course. Harry smiled, as he might well have done. I'd raised my voice, risen to his bait. But I was angry, for God's sake. Rightly so. Though I didn't want to acknowledge to myself that I'd faded in and then out of something, I'd been far away from Harry and the gallery and everything, drifting off somewhere. Terry was watching us.

I stood up, shakily, but with enough energy to have Harry step back a pace or two.

'You haven't lived, Harry. You've seen nothing, been educated to nothing. Your arse-wipe newspaper needs you for show, everyone else has a Harry. Can I buy you in kit form?'

I'd lowered my voice, but Harry's smile had disappeared. Dried up, I should say, it was rather like that. I hadn't meant at all to say what I'd said, but there was no residue of guilt, thank God, no feeling that I should apologise or retract anything. I saw the little fat boy no one would talk to in the schoolyard pull his soiled Yankness over his head and his Mom said night-night and tucked him up. Harry wilted visibly, head down.

'Rude and vulgar,' he trailed after him. 'The slip is showing.'

I barely heard him.

The crowd was dispersing. I suppose I'd helped them along, come to that. The old crip getting stroppy again, time to leave. I huddled a bit myself, behind a dodgy damp canapé and a fresh big iced gin. Harry was talking to someone, keeping his dignity rather well, I should have said. I was a disgust – John's use of the word. He used to describe Francis as a disgust when in his more Bacchanalian episodes. I felt, absurdly, like crying. Whenever I felt like this, painting helped. I wanted – Harry would no doubt have said needed – to get back to my studio. Terry was wandering around, happy with himself. I tapped his shoulder.

'Give my regards to your good wife.'

'Are you off? I thought we might have dinner later, a few...'

'No thank you, Terry. I'm plunging rather nastily into my cups. Another time. And thank you most sincerely for everything. Wonderful.'

I held his hand and shook it vigorously. Terry knew me long enough to let me off when I wanted to go. I looked around and saw a generous rash of red spots. Terry said, looking with me:

'You've done well already. Will you come in during the week and we'll run over some things?'

'I hate business, Terry. But I will, of course. I should say something to him, Terry, shouldn't I? I insulted him, lost it. He hasn't lived. Not like me, is it? Or is it?'

Terry, like the gent he is, didn't play stupid and act as if he'd seen-no-evil-heard-no-evil. He raised his eyebrows. He looked like a brush handle with a worn layer of bristles on top. His breath smelled, oddly, of mint.

'He's not the most loved, I know that. But he's young.'

'Maybe that's what I dislike about him. He'll call

me a prick in his column. I'll sue.'

We both laughed. But I couldn't rid myself of a gnat-like itch, an irritation of spirit, call it what you will. I shook Terry's hand again and did the sort of social choreography that had me out on the street in the chill dry river wind alongside Harry, God love him, both of us goodnighting Terry with waves.

Porky on pate, Laocoon-ed by my damp scarf, stick conducting traffic, I stump-legged my way across the street almost by Harry's wounded side. I walk fast. Harry wasn't going my way. At length, I had to stop, pull myself up to a lopsided height and shout after him. An elderly queen shouting after a fat young man in a street gorged with sex-shops, as it happens. Very nice.

'You have my apologies, Harry!'

He kept going. This was too ridiculous. Then he turned.

'Have a drink with me,' I said. Heads turned in the street. Very silly, all of it. But Harry hadn't lived. That was all, curiously, I could think of. He walked back to me, rather tight-lipped and prissy, I might add. But he walked back.

'I was unconscionably rude,' I said. Harry, being American, would have trouble with unconscionably. I stuck out a hand. The cold air was full of fat white seabirds that should have been in their beds. Some of them circled us like angels and barked. Harry looked very small and lost.

126

'I don't believe in keeping a grudge with artists,' Harry said. Nice of him, I thought, very uncharitably. 'It's not the first time someone's taken a shot.' He was game, I'll give him that.

We shook hands. That's what gentlemen do. I offered him the drink again. He looked at me as if I'd propositioned him. Then I could see little gears cogging up behind his eyes, little men running backwards and forwards across his retina carrying messages, or votes perhaps, one way or the other. He'd boast that old whatsizface had tried him up. You know, the painter. Queer as a three-pound. Quasimodo, with a cane. Paints Bacon lookalikes and says he doesn't. Him. Good for a tea-break giggle with the girls in the canteen, or wherever Harry sits at trough. He might even call in the rag's brief and see if it'd be kosher to call me a queer. Which it wouldn't these days. I hate the word Gay, myself. Makes it appear that all of us are happy. Which we are not. Harry yawned. He'd made a decision, or the little scuttling men had.

'Where?'

'My place,' I said, and saw him wince. You really must see the Minotaur's lair, Harry, I thought maliciously. Do some living. Besides, it's a story. The artist's lair.

'The spider's web,' Harry said.

'Something like that.'

'Are you inviting me back to your place?'

'You make it sound like I've just shown you my prick, Harry. No, actually. I want you – need you – to see my studio. I want to show you where everything takes place, as it were.'

That was different. Harry could see what was what, he's not stupid. I wanted him to see what I believed about the human figure, blah-blah, and so on. I explained all of this as we walked. His notebook flagged out of his arse pocket like a rent-boy's menu handkerchief. He actually helped me down and up some quaintly Georgian steps. We cruised along the quays in slow motion. Or so it must have appeared to the rest of the bustling younger world. Dying is merely getting old very fast, John used to say. When he could still speak. On the way, we collected cigarettes, a bottle of plonk.

My door. Big and pompous with knowledge of its preservation order, my Georgian castle towers over our demolished street. The sound of African music one side, the odour of Chinese cooking the other, and always a Gauguin of colourful women walking up and down carrying bags and small children. They chatter and laugh and show big white teeth. Now and then an African in an expensive suit and immaculate white shirt will stand and look up and down the street. The women know me. The Chinese keep to themselves. The grandmother speaks no English, a wizened doll of

128

a woman drying like vellum in the back room, you can see here every time the door to the kitchen swings open. I remember the Italian chippers with their Pope pictures and the sound of new chips when they'd crash into the boiling fat. Changes. The odour of hashish drifts like a gas on the wind.

I fiddle the majestic useless key in the lock. The big door's paint is peeling redly. The knocker, brassy smooth, reflects every light in the street.

'After you, Harry.'

Harry is carrying the bags like a good boy. We enter the catastrophe of my room and I turn on the light. A naked bulb, of course. There are my familiars, my wrecked couch, my crushed armchairs, the drink-sodden Turkish carpet, the retreating wallpaper. I indicate the couch to Harry. If he only knew the celebrity arse that's snuggled down there, he'd be grateful. More for the column. But knowing things isn't really living, is it? There's more.

Over the plonk from relatively clean glasses, we create little damp patches of silence. Harry's eyes wander around the room, going off on their own. I let them. I watch Harry. I study the tightness of the fabric of his pants over his fat knees, the way, I suppose, Michaelangelo studied the folds of fabric in his day. Not that I like Harry's fat knees, God help us. Harry takes everything in. He reads the spines of my few books by tilting his head. He spots the book, coffee-

129

table size, on Velasquéz.

'That's from the Bacon set-up. The reconstructed flat.'

'No, that's the original.'

Drinkenly impressed, Harry actually went over to have a look at it. That was the loneliest, the saddest thing I could ever have imagined him doing and I didn't give him credit for much. He was like a curious child. A man-child. A living ambiguity between maturity and childhood. Ideas for a study formed in my head. Then Harry leaned up and away from the book, which I'd bought, as it turned out, for fifty pee out of a basket a month ago.

The silence, as Harry turned around and turned around like a figure in a music-box, was a colour all of its own. A texture, too. Like sandpaper. The old irritation came back. I wanted Harry to be more curious and then I'd show him what he wanted – needed – to see. Sure enough,

'And where, like, do you work?'

'Back in there,' I said carelessly.

'I really would like to see the studio.'

'Your-eyes-only status, Harry. Have I your word?'

Harry was hooked. He reached round for his notebook but I nodded my head seriously like a teacher who'd received the wrong answer. He understood, or the child in him did. I stood up wearily. How much, after all, can you expect another to

130

understand you?

Behind a heavy red curtain, mottled at the hem with rat munchings, I opened my studio door. Another naked light bulb blew out upon a long room full of paints, brushes in tins, bottles of turps, easels, clothes, rolled paper, big housepainter-sized brushes, empty wine bottles, objects under white sheets and God knew what else. There were no windows, which was just as well of late. At the shadowy end of the room was the fire escape door, which also did for deliveries at all hours.

'Funny smell,' said Harry.

'Paint and things. The usual.'

Harry planted himself awkwardly on a paint-mottled rickety stool. I put on an apron. I steadied a large canvas on its legs. Harry got up, as I knew he would, and took a peek.

'Part of my Resurrection series, Harry. Driving me ga-ga. It needs life, the human shape rising from the earth sort of thing. Won't be a tick.'

Harry nodded and grunted. The dark tones of the work so far revealed very little. But the hint was there, a mass tissue rising agonisingly from the earth itself. I might just chance something with this one, I thought. I might let it flow a little. Like water.

'Definitely,' said Harry. He was getting just a tad wall-eyed now, our Harry. He phlunked his big tumorous arse across the little round stool. It disappeared up inside him. Billy Bunter wrapped in Old Glory. He slugged his wine back and peered about him again. I leaned into the canvas and pretended not to look at him. In fact I couldn't keep my eyes off him now.

'What sorta life?'

'I don't know, Harry. Something natural. Just a hint of movement. A gesture.'

Harry didn't understand, and indicated this with a lardy frown. It made him look even younger. I'd conveyed the impression that I was using him as a model and that made him drunkenly smug. This was fame indeed, for Harry; how the coffee cups would chatter now! He began to straighten himself up, as clearly he thought a good sitter should. Harry was, quaintly, Old School, if you follow.

'You're obsessed with the human figure,' Harry said. I suppose it was a question. By now I had angled myself in towards the canvas like a truly inspired painter. Harry, watching me, would have seen that. He found it difficult to sit up straight and hold his glass in his hand. The wine was spilling, though he didn't notice it. Dark red on cream white.

'It is all we are, Harry. That absurd pronged image. Then it disintegrates. Symbol of time itself. Loosen yourself a little, Harry.'

I didn't make sense even to myself. But that was unimportant. Harry was hypnotised. Every word I said now, every gesture I made, would sit like a jewel in the rubbish-heap of Harry's critical mind. I felt inexplicably sad. Are all critics merely lonely children no one'll play with? Is art itself such a sad thing? Am I someone's fretful lost child?

A lump formed in my throat, a tightness that seemed to rise out of my chest. As the lump grew, it pulled its energy from my hands. The brush slowed, got stuck in its own paint. I stood back from the work. I took a depth breath. Harry was staring at some point on the floor. I recovered myself. Whatever had hovered round my soul had flown.

'Must have models,' I heard Harry say. He smiled, but it was like a great toothachy thing, bending his face. 'I really liked your work tonight. It's just like, well, I guess we're kinda all Bacon-ed out....'

'The models are all around you, Harry. Pull off one of those drapes. Carefully, now.'

I'd paid enough for them, God knows. And they wouldn't last. I'd end up having to pay to have them taken back. Dark doings at the back door. So I had to make as much use of them while I....

Harry screamed. Well, a loudly amplified rat's squeak, if you can imagine. A sound as if his very soul were being dragged across a bed of nails. His hands in the air like that, the expression on his face as his flabby mouth opened, the glass tumbling over and over in the air, spouting wine like blood everywhere as if he'd been shot, his body arched backwards and upwards from the waist. You couldn't ask for better.

I worked quickly, filling my head with a sort of snapshot, a still, of Harry's St Vitus' hysterics. The human figure repelled him, obviously. Headless, armless and legless it was broken down to its workable minimal centre, the focus point from out of which emotion was drawn, shaped, angled; but you couldn't explain that to Harry. I don't like too much whiteness, it hints at leprosy, and the effect of darkening and withering to indicate decay, an eating away, is achieved by pouring a little petrol, an eggcupful, over an incision in the flesh and then setting it alight. The flesh will crisp and darken. Takes a while, and it's smelly, but it works. I felt confident about the Resurrection works. Harry's little agony would pass, but I'd captured it, at least in the rough. I could touch it up. The vomiting I most certainly did not need.

Or is it want?

(for Brian and Doreen Wynn)

# Master Foynes
# His Galliard

'Which danceth galliards in your amorous eyes...'
                              Sir John Davies: *Orchestra*'

She sat, uncomfortably hot, in the front row.

Several feet in front of her, three middle-aged gentlemen and a grossly overweight woman sawed away in a melancholy fashion at a set of viols, archaic instruments which, Davina had assured her, were copies of the originals. Davina had a concerned interest in Early Music and she trusted her verdicts. The quartet was called Oddes Boddes and they were, Davina had said, renowned. The musicians sat as if the burden of their accumulated musical learning had made them sad.

The music so far was slow and quaintly melancholy. The building was suitable, high-ceilinged, stone, old, with long narrow windows that looked full of black glass now against the early night. There was a good crowd; the room was hot, and programmes flapped like slim glossy fans. A woman sat patiently near the closed exit door, behind a table loaded with Oddes Boddes CDs and cassettes.

No one in the audience was particularly young. Impeccably dressed, one or two men actually wearing dickies, each face determined and solemn under the ancient music. Davina sat beside her; the shiny, purple flower-patterned dress this evening, Davina's fat calves muttering under the wet-looking fabric. Davina had chins. She was utterly respectable and ran a tiny shop which sold genuine native brasswork from somewhere in the mountains of Tibet or some such. She had been drawn to Davina at first because she too was English and there was the stubborn schoolgirlish silliness of exile.

Davina's husband, divorcing her, had left her two teenage sons and the shop over which Davina had a modest but eloquent apartment. He had been Irish, wild, a part-time fisherman and bog-wood sculptor. The Irish in this part of the island were different from the rest, tainted by Spanish and French and Elizabethan English blood.

Davina irritated her with the sort of posed attentiveness – so she believed it to be – before the group of musicians. Perhaps she fancied the bearded, balding one who grimaced sensuously as he dug against the strings with his bow. Davina was a difficult woman. Even announcing she had cancer – had she really announced it that far evening? – had been a particularly Davina sort of thing to do; drinks had been served, curtains drawn, music put on. Lute music; Italian Renaissance. The gentle plucking scored itself around Davina's quietly-voiced sentence of self-death.

'You can dump my ashes in the river!' Her conclusion had ended, it seemed, on a clear, prolonged F-sharp minor.

As Oddes Boddes vibrated and hummed over a refreshingly lusty galliard, she remembered that night vividly. Rain had pelted the big windows behind the blue velveteen curtains of Davina's cosy main room. She'd done some renovating since her husband had moved out; she detested the new and garish apartments being built all over the old town. Old bones, she remarked, ordered to hold up a garish, livid-looking architectural skin; all those lurid pinks and cheap yellows. Davina and she had often discussed what was happening to the town, as if they were natives; not chubby, lightly-monied women who had, at some point, found life utterly unliveable in their own country, fleeing here to the lip of the cold Atlantic, panicked and breathing hard.

Still, that evening had been a bit of a start. Davina had grown plumper, softer, the medication doing this and that to her metabolism. The months had become a year. The year had become two, and here they were. Davina's skin had tightened and become blotchy and increasingly she was challenged by dizziness and sudden weakness. But she still looked at men and talked in a refined bawdy sort of way when she'd had a few drinks. Her death, her not being there, would be intolerable.

'Lucy,' Davina had said, resting her ringed hand on Lucy's staunch knee. 'We're not kids anymore, so do stop sniffling for my bloody sake and have another gin. Death is a feature of our lives, now drink up.'

Lucy did not possess such strength.

'It would have been better had you married, Lucy dear,' Davina had said. on some other occasion of blubbering and disgrace. 'You're far too sensitive to life.'

These days Lucy had become absent-minded, losing keys, having other drivers honk angrily at her as she drove stupidly on familiar streets. The town seemed to have more people suddenly, the streets narrower. Sometimes the thought of Davina – the conjuring up of her face or some joke she'd made – threw her in to an irrational and troublesome panic.

Oddes Boddes played on. Sacrilegiously, someone coughed. A piece ended. The bearded, balding musician stood up, smiling, bowing.

'A piece, ladies and gentlemen, to close with, entitled 'Master Foynes His Galliard,' written...'

'...by William Jopson,' Davina muttered, quite distinctly, a smile of sorts fixed on the musician, anticipating every word, a sort of prompter-after-the-fact.

'...for the son, we believe, of the third Earl of Lychenfield...

'...who was executed in fifteen-eighty-eight!' Davina finished with a wheezy flourish that made the musician bow towards her.

'Now there's a lady who knows her music,' said the musician gallantly, and the audience in the first rows looked in Davina's direction and snickered jealously but politely. The musician, naturally, bowed.

Lucy looked at Davina's profile. Handsome all her life, never beautiful. Perhaps handsome was better. Lucy remembered that she herself had once been described as very good-looking by a man who had then tried to undress her, roughly and without any sort of love, in the front seats of his car and whose name she'd forgotten soon afterwards. A few men had flitted through her life. Some names stayed with her, associated not with faces but with vague black evening settings, false and unsteady, like background sets in an ancient black-and-white movie. One man had made her cry out during sex. Another had made her giggle. There was nothing more. She was certain that love, for example, had never come into it. Perhaps what she'd had was to real love what handsome was to beautiful.

'Dreadfully sad story,' Davina whispered to her behind a programme.

'What is?'

'What happened to his son. Terrible.'

'Oh,' said Lucy. 'It was The Earl of Lychenfield's son who was executed. Oh, terrible times.'

'No, no,' said Davina. 'His son was drowned. Here. In Ireland.' Davina jabbed a thick forefinger for emphasis at the polished yellow boards of the floor. The first slow, sombre phrases of the galliard moved off at their elegant pace; a little decorated boat of sound pushing out from the platform. Lucy felt unreasonably anguished. Behind her hand, she questioned Davina.

'Lychenfield was executed for treason or some such. Putting down a rebellion. The usual. Wasn't harsh enough, so I'm told.'

'The poor man,' Lucy sighed. The music crooned outwards, upwards, into every cranny and plaster-crack in the mid-Victorian hall. Lucy wanted to dance, to sway sedately at the fingertips of young Master Foynes. A thought unsettled her. Unsettled, that is, the harmless dream the music had produced.

'His son was a child,' Davina said, reading her thoughts. Sometimes, Lucy had noted before now, her friend could read people's thoughts. It was uncanny and very unmannerly. 'A boy. Not more than a boy. Only child. Dreadful! Now do let's listen.'

The galliard moved over into a minor key, swung out again, repeated itself; woven through it all was grief and joy, joy and grief, innocence and agony and death. Lucy wondered whether she'd locked and shuttered her gallery properly. A sudden wave of unreasonable panic struck her, washed over her, trundled on. All those cheap and talentless paintings and drawings; every now and then someone wandered in off a wet street and considered them all with exaggerated patience and purchased one. Out of kindness, Lucy often thought. Out of pity. A blousey, middle-aged – lost, fading, hopeless – but respectable woman taking their money, fawning slightly, wrapping the best-I-can-do work of half-art and letting her accent do the rest. Her accent had an odd effect on people here, she'd noticed long ago. It attracted them, they patronised her. Elderly women tried to prune their vowels and sculpt their consonants when speaking to her; chip off whole healthy chunks of rural Irish accent in her presence. They tried to imitate her. At first, it was dreadful. Gradually she'd adjusted to the masque presented before her at the simplest tea-morning, the most ridiculously mundane meeting in the street. Why, she wondered, did so many of this town's women want to be her?

Finding Davina had been a miracle, a true miracle. Lucy did not believe in God. She surrounded herself with God-by-other-means, the soft alluring trinketry of tiny fat brass Buddhas to hold incense sticks, an accumulation of rather dull and silent crystals, books on 'rearing' her inner child, books on astrology – she had a chart done, of course, on Davina's insistence –

141

and a do-it-yourself rune-casting kit. She had cassette-recordings of whales and dolphins breathing or signalling underwater and one particularly rare one of a Siberian shaman imitating a wolf for hunting-magic. The shaman's notes did something to her head. She couldn't bear to play the recording for too long. The shaman's weird notes slipped inside the chamber of her skull and disturbed something balanced and vital there. But it all showed there was a different world to the one in which she had her existence and that was what was important.

Davina had come in to her life just when she'd been considering closing down the gallery – returning all of those scrappy earnest paintings and drawings to their anxious fathers and mothers, burning her own – and going back to England.

'There's nothing there,' Davina had explained. 'It's all gone. Anything that was good is gone.'

'That can't be entirely true,' Lucy had argued. 'I was born there, that's where I come from.'

'That doesn't mean anything,' Davina had said. 'Even the place you were born in – what are you now – fifty? Even where you were born's disappeared.'

'Fifty in April. You have family here. It's different for you.'

'Take my ex-husband then. Start a family of your own with him.'

They'd both laughed, then, that long-ago evening,

grateful to have a bottle of red wine with which to dilute the lonely seriousness of their lives. Letters from friends had, over time, confirmed, more or less what Davina had said. Their tone, or lack of tone. Their England was a past swallowed up by events and circumstances no one would make the effort to explain.

'You see, we were never England's type,' Davina had said that evening; and Lucy had thought she'd known what she'd meant. All those girls she'd grown up with, the same good schools, now married, plump and children-weary but getting on with it in a recognised and admired way; never for her, all that. But she'd never been adventurous, either. Lucy had found herself merely confused.

Davina had had children but that hadn't been the same, she'd had them wildly, drunkenly, with a wild drinking Irishman with unkempt hair and an unwashed beard. Not the same at all! Not England's type at all!

An ache remained, the tooth pulled but a little of the root still there, nagging. She knew that Davina, for all her years in exile, rarely if ever listened to Irish radio. She followed The Archers every day – you couldn't speak when it was on – and discussed the characters as if they were real people. BBC Radio 4 news broadcasts were the only ones she'd listen to. And BBC radio's glossy dramatisations of novels.

'They do their research, Lucy. They get it right.

These Sundays it's War and Peace and in the battle scenes you have horses neighing and the sound of cartwheels and all sorts of things.'

The galliard to the dead child swung out into a new and happier tune; Lucy felt her eyelids parting. Had she been dozing? Dreamily she sought out the forms of the musicians and, finding them, heard the new tune's parts repeating themselves, heard the note of dead childhood making itself heard. Jopson knew how to write music, she thought. He knew how to use music as a net to catch emotions; and ghosts, and the anguish of dead children.

'Oh!'

Lucy had uttered the cry politely, if involuntarily, under her breath. But its urgency made Davina's head turn. Lucy blushed. Davina looking at her could sometimes have that effect; she blushed under those suddenly stern eyes.

'Are you all right?'

'Yes, of course,' said Lucy.

'Quiet!' someone hissed a row or two behind them.

Evenings such as these, Lucy told herself, always held within their grasp the particles of all sorts of disasters. One could never be sure. She felt trapped, watched. The galliard moved into its final round, easing slowly downwards, it seemed, big treacly black notes slithering down the hot, thick air. The tune ended with such brutally sad beauty that her eyes brimmed over with hot unstoppable tears. She applauded until her hands hurt. She wanted to slap away the sound of a terrible sadness. Davina applauded far too politely. The sadness came and went, came and went, in and out the ups and downs of the applause. The musicians rose, bowed, and the audience rose with them. Now on her feet, Lucy felt the tears drying on her cheeks and was grateful.

'Absolutely marvellous!' Davina said; then, quite loudly, 'Bravo! Bravo! Encore!'

Lucy didn't want to hear any more. What she'd heard was quite enough. Too much music like that could not be good for you; it went in, seeped in, to places in the heart which were far too private and which, up until the moment of their invasion, had been guarded ferociously from the world. The music was a taste of a greater and less controllable hurt. A hurt world-deep and in which everyone shared sooner or later.

The musicians too had had enough. They trundled off the platform with studied, disciplined decorum, hoisting and cradling their suddenly babyishly plump instruments.

'No question, but I must have one of their CDs,' said Davina, with alarming and unmatchable enthusiasm, and vanished.

Lucy was left to make her way along the row of seats as best she could. People recognised her, saluted, said polite quiet things. Lucy overheard the greetings and friendly comments as if she were eavesdropping on a private conversation. Her eyes felt gritty and dry. Davina's eldest son, Matthew, was standing by the mock-Gothic exit door. Davina always called him Matty. He's come to take us home, Lucy thought, and brightened. Matthew was in his early twenties, dark-eyed and mischievous. The Irish in him. I'll bet he has the ladies, Lucy thought, finding a bawdy smile on her face. There was something fabulously bawdy and brazen and life-loving about the young; they had the power to restore, to resurrect. Lucy occasionally caught herself envying the young, but not in a common, middleaged, spiteful way.

She hooked her arm into Matthew's and the young man, out-of-place by virtue of his age and his zipper jacket and his deliberately shaven head, edged into the shadows.

'Car's downstairs,' muttered Matthew. Then he raised his head and looked over the crowd into the far blank wall. His face wore no expression Lucy could decipher. She knew, then, that Davina had asked him to come and collect them. He wanted to be elsewhere. Suddenly she was ashamed of herself and she allowed her arm to snake furtively out of his. They stood together, miles and years apart, deeply embarrassed.

On the drive across the town, Davina kept up a tiring and unanswerable commentary on the evening's music. She'd bought an Oddes Boddes CD entitled Alle in a Rounde. 'Their first,' she qualified huffily, unwrapping it violently in the dim half-light of the vehicle. The streets of the town had fallen into their usual blighted, gaudily-lit stupor; young drunks vomited on the pavements and their companions urinated openly against the wheels of parked cars. The wet warm air was full of the odour of dead carnivals and frantic, unimaginable festivals that seemed to be going on just out of sight, at the farthest edge of human perception. Lucy looked out and saw what she saw and recalled the perfect rural silence of these streets all those years ago when she'd first arrived.

'Now that's bloody awful!' Davina shouted in her ear. They sat together in the back seat. Matthew's neck was pitted, Lucy noted for no reason, with the ravages of acne. Davina was turning her head slowly as they drove past a very old stone building which was draped in construction fencing and had red-painted Keep Out signs hanging all over it.

'Too much of that nonsense in this town! Shouldn't be allowed.'

'Mother,' said Matthew; it came out as a very English sigh.

'We should write a letter. Someone should.'

'Pointless,' Lucy said. She felt, suddenly, weary and peevish. She wanted to disagree with things.

'Then I'll write a letter,' Davina challenged. 'One can't just feel helpless.'

'No one cares,' said Lucy.

'I care,' said Davina. The car filled with silence then; just as, had it fallen into the river, it might have filled with water.

Getting out of the car, Davina seemed to stumble; a short, half-stepped, half-danced little balancing act. Lucy grabbed her by the arm; she could feel, under the ample jacket and all the rest, the hard ruthlessness of bone. The flesh was flabby and gelatinous, as if all substance was being dissolved from it.

'You're a pal,' said Davina. 'Ta muchly.'

Matthew drove off quickly. The sound of the car was in Lucy's ears as Davina fumbled over a set of electronic security buttons.

'Is the shop all right?'

'Yes,' said Lucy. 'The shop's fine.'

'Different times we live in,' said Davina.

She always made Lucy look and wouldn't look herself. She pushed then, and the heavy wooden door hummed and clicked open. The odour of frying and hot grease mixed with incense came down the stairs. Davina, Lucy noticed, took deep breaths to help her up the thin staircase.

The two women ascended loudly in pitch-blackness, one behind the other, the sounds their clothing made brushing against the walls resembled something tearing. The air of the narrow stairway felt cold and wet against Lucy's cheek, as if a ghostly

148

breath hovered beside her. Davina groaned quietly with the effort of the stairs. Then she was at the top and a gentle reddish light from a hooded and slightly Oriental corner lamp washed the walls. Lucy found herself stranded in the middle of Davina's main room, standing more or less in the very centre of a Muslim prayer-mat. Behind her, an electric fire came on with a nudge from a thermostat and her hands began to warm. Davina had swept herself quickly into her bedroom.

The door was open. Lucy glimpsed, just for a brief moment and in a spasm of shame, the unsettling ivory scalp of Davina's hairless head. Off came the wig she'd worn out; on went another just like it. When Davina came back into the room she looked thinner and tired, as if she'd done battle with some invisible draining thing in the violated privacy of her bedroom. She fiddled and fussed, making appropriate noises, over the shiney plastic lid of her CD player; soon enough, the viols and other reconstructed instruments of Oddes Boddes' armoury sounded out over the shadowy country of the warming room.

'Drinks,' said Davina, to no one in particular. It was an instruction to herself to undertake another task; as Lucy watched her, Davina slid gracefully from one side of the room to another, to a drinks' cabinet, sorted out glasses, produced bottles. The speed with which she moved seemed to indicate, or recall,

149

vigorous good health. Perhaps that was the idea; perhaps disease could be wished away.

'What'll it be, Luce? And do sit down.'

'Gin and tonic,' Lucy replied, but with someone else's voice. The voice, when she remembered it, of a little girl lost in a crowd. The room seemed suddenly to be full of people who longed to say things and couldn't. It was a curious sensation. Lucy wondered for a moment whether she was coming down with something. The old music flooded the room, assumed an almost visible shape, a sort of thin blue cloud which drifted over the wicker chairs – genuine Edwardian Raj – and the wide and bulky futon concealed under a vast woven depiction of two smiling howda-ed elephants raising their trunks at each other and standing on their hind legs. One of the elephants seemed to be reading a page of The Irish Times that was draped over the back back of the futon. Davina had been doing the crossword. There were a great number of blanks.

Incongruous, Lucy thought. The word made a metallic sound in her head. She feel ashamed of herself for thinking up such a word.

Davina gestured to the floor. The prayer-mat disappeared completely under them and they sat cross-legged like much younger women. They sipped their drinks for a time without saying anything. Davina brought the G&T. The mischievous random ticking of the electric fire and the deep plaint of Oddes Boddes seemed, for a time, to be enough for them. Just beyond the draped windows the black fast river rattled and sloshed over hidden, terrible rocks, then ducked slyly under weary bridges and sniggered under the ancient foundations of the town. Everything here is floating on water, Lucy thought, lulled by the curtained cackling of the river; we are floating, like Venice, waiting to be drowned again in the sea. The river crashed under the mediaeval terraces, fidgeted into the arms of the sea. The air was full of water; it rained, there were soft enveloping fogs, whole clouds hissed over the city like a smothering gauze. And we are water, Lucy thought, and the moon is our mother; she had several engaging books on the relationship. Pretty esoteric things were not to be discussed with just anyone; Davina understood, however.

But nothing had hurled itself out of the moon, or the sea, or out of the sun, or raged up out of the river or the earth to stiffle Davina's slow, patient cancer. No sacred stone nor flashing crystal, no scented chanting, no barefooted circular dance, nor runic consultation had even so much as gestured towards a return to good health, an end to disease. Lucy felt chilled by a sudden sense of hopelessness; as if all possibility of belief or faith in anything, however glorious or decadent, was gone. She saw in Davina's gradual wasting a more subtle wasting in herself.

Davina had closed her eyes. Her hand steadied the

glass whose base rested now on the floor. She was humming along to the music of Oddes Boddes.

'God's Body,' Lucy said out loud for no reason. Davina smiled.

'The things you come out with, Luce. Really, I don't know.' Davina said without opening here eyes. Her head had dropped forward; she spoke into her large breasts.

'It's what it means,' said Lucy, feeling fragile, lost. She could not take her eyes of Davina; her gaze coasted over the woman, every ripple of clothing, the macabre wig, the blotched but stubborn palour of the facial skin, the thin wrist ending in the sparkle of the glass.

'Oddes Boddes,' Davina murmured. Her voice had become deep and clogged with sleep. 'They were odd bodies, too, weren't they?' Davina giggled.

Lucy heard the river sounds and the old music fold over into each other. She closed her eyes and saw how dark and infinite was the universe, how close, how far its stars and suns. She opened her eyes, sipped violently at her drink. Davina rallied suddenly, lifted her head.

'I sat down to have a nice chat, and look what happens,' Davina said. She could still manage a radiant smile, Lucy thought. She was a handsome woman; what is beauty?

'You're just tired.'

'Well, I'm not just tired. The drugs, damn them.

They catch up on me. My mind wants to keep going but the body lets it down. Lets me down.'

Lucy looked into her glass. A car roared by on the street, an ugly, snarling noise, a wild animal noise. The world was, in its own way, a dreadful place.

'Lucy.'

Davina's fingertips were cold and sharp on Lucy's skin. Lucy didn't look up. The music and the river joined hands. All at once, by a fingers' touch, a depressing weight lowered itself over Lucy's heart. She felt her breathing tighten.

'Lucy, there are things we really must talk about.'

'I can't,' said Lucy. She felt poisoned and sad, as if Davina's fingers had injected a deep and unredeemable melancholy into her blood.

'If I can, you can. They're the rules.'

'Don't, please. It's not as simple as that.'

Davina removed her fingers. Lucy dragged at her drink, wished heartily she had a whole bottle of the stuff, a bottle of gin, neat, to Hell with it.

'I'm not afraid, Lucy. Nor should you be.'

'I don't care whether you're afraid or not. We aren't all of us so bloody brave. It's silly. Silly to be so brave. No – it's selfish, that's what it is.'

'There are things I have to talk about, Lucy,' said Davina, her voice maternal, warm, protecting. 'There are things, as you can imagine, that I want you to do for me.'

153

'Forget it. I'm not listening.'

'Now who's being selfish? Think of the boys.'

'They're grown up.'

'They are not.'

The music and the river formed a liquid current of sound that moved around the room, and they breathed it in without noticing. Davina's voice had risen sharply; a musical note. Then it recovered itself, tidied itself up and fell away again.

'I don't want them to remember any ugliness,' Davina said. Her voice was tired, deep, and soothing. 'I want life to be good for them. All their memories pleasant ones.'

Lucy unfolded her legs. They ached softly with cramp. Her glass was empty. She wanted to be out of Davina's apartment, out in the fresh cold wet air of the world. Then all that was bad and sad and oppressive would simply blow away. Disappear, like a sad song ending, fading, stopping. She longed for the neon colour, the artificial jubilance of the streets; the youth, the laughter, the shouts of young girls, the taunts of young men in their drunkenness and lust. In the streets there was forgetfulness and no death.

Lucy stood up. Davina looked up at her, surprised.

'We'll talk again, Lucy. We must, that's all.'

Lucy said nothing. For a moment or two she readied herself in the middle of the floor. The CD had ended. The noise of the river beyond the window was colourless and cold. People drowned in rivers and in other people.

'Yes, we'll talk again,' said Lucy. 'When I'm not so stressed.'

The world was stressed. So was the age. There was neither happiness nor hope, only the comforts and disguises of anxiety. Lucy had books on this too.

Davina stood in front of her, her eyes fading in a wet lustre of discomfort. She embraced Lucy and Lucy felt the hot iron-smelling brush of Davina's breath on her cheek. There was something voluptuously decayed about Davina's breath; a terrible seductiveness, the warm promise of a darker world. And that tang of iron, the odour of hot old blood. Lucy held Davina in a brief but tight embrace and then let her go. She felt a deep and impossible pity for the woman. It was bound up with her own feelings, less easily explained, of loss and chilly anguish. Lucy felt the frail but majestic power of Davina's illness as their arms parted; an invisible hooked line strung between them.

'I'll call, probably Tuesday,' said Lucy. She smiled, as much to steady herself as to reassure Davina. Davina's face had closed against her; a tightening of the pale lips, a stretching of the skin under the eyes, barely discernible symptoms of rejection and dismissal.

'Tuesday,' Davina nodded.

There was nothing more to be said. Lucy made her

way down the dark stairwell – Davina hadn't bothered to turn on the light at the top of the stairs – and as she reached the front door and opened it, she heard Davina bolting and double-locking herself into her apartment above. Lucy opened the door and luxuriated in the soft wet touch of the street breeze, felt the salty bite of the breeze borne up the street from the open sea, over the docks and the sleeping small vessels hugging the stone harbour walls as they had done for centuries. She looked up and saw the red light in Davina's apartment go out.

She moved off up the street, feeling the gentle tug of the medieval gradient push her shoulders forward. The old Protestant church tower clock sounded midnight; she thought of those ancient, leaning, neglected tombstones, all bearing names from a country which was near and yet far and in which they no longer carried any resonance and where their meaning had been forgotten. A noisy gang of young people, dressed in jeans and sloppy pullovers, some of them carrying cans of beer, made a mock dance, a skipping sort of Morris, and chanted their way past her. Oh, you don't see me! You don't see me at all! Lucy thought to herself and smiled.

She stood perfectly still in the middle of the road, a respectable, flamboyant, heavy-looking woman who took care of herself, allowing a crowded taxi to cruise slowly across her path. In the back seat of the taxi, a young couple giggled and snuggled into each other. Time means nothing, Lucy thought now; time is one thing and then another. Time is neither life nor death.

She moved over a bridge. The footpath was narrow and she hugged the stone parapet. Sad young people had, on occasions when the moon hid her face, jumped from this parapet into the cold swollen waters of the river below. Most had never been found.

She stood in the middle of the bridge, at its highest point over the river. Now she was suspended between heaven and earth, all that mediaeval man could do, she had read, to imitate such a miracle. The noise of the river was loud here and relentless. She looked up into a suddenly clear sky of frantically winking stars and a whisp of crescent moon.

Lucy held her arms outstretched away from her sides and turned round once, twice, three times, feeling slightly dizzy when she stopped, found herself giggling to herself with a swift rush of new blood into her face. You are utterly ridiculous, she told herself. But she was not unhappy.

The old galliard was in her head now, its strains taking on a texture she hadn't noticed before. Now she heard the innocence and joy and young energy Jopson had translated into the music. The world is of our making, the music said; it does not exist without us. She looked and saw that she was alone on the bridge accept for the faint small figure of a young boy

157

standing at a distance.

Yet he was not standing, but dancing, reaching into the air for stars, catching them in his small frantic fingers; and the music in her head made him dance. And he was full of joy and content with his child's world and he was a child and did not know death.

(for Saoirse, μψ δαυγητερ)

# Vacansou

*'Qui meurt de mort violente doit rester entre vie et mort jusqu'à ce que se soit écoulé le temps qu'il avait naturellement à vivre.'*

Anatole Le Braz: *La Légende de la Mort*

She parked their car, feeling only a stingy twinge under her arm as she pulled on the steering wheel. They came up to the single-storeyed house in late sunlight, their shadows long and light on the gravel. The house was surrounded by bushes and small trees and there were hills and sharp toothy outcrops on the horizon. The sky was a late blue speckled with gold and white clouds. She got out of the car and he started unloading bags and she put transparent stickers over the headlights that would adjust the beams to French levels, up and down. The sound of the gravel under their feet was monstrous in the stillness.

Inside the house there were rooms to inspect. There was, as she'd expected, the low unease of being in someone else's house. She saw the TV set, the stove, the sink, mirrors, cutlery and all the time he was opening drawers and the fridge and listing loudly to himself what was absent. They needed milk, eggs, butter. They needed a hundred things. There was a note neat-printed in a lemon-coloured envelope from the owners of the house. There were various keys in the envelope too. She used her schoolgirl French to decipher which was for what. He was out in the back garden by then and had poured himself a glass of wine from the half dozen or so they'd brought with them. You won't need it, she'd told him. But he'd bought them anyway. She felt light-headed and asked him to pour her a glass of wine. He came in from the garden and told her he'd seen a hedgehog under some hedges and he wondered if there might also be foxes. *Or wolves*, he said, *you just never know*.

She was a small woman with a girl's figure though she wouldn't ever be a girl again and her grey-blonde hair was coming out in slivers and soon it might all come out. She had blue eyes which, he told her now and then, were the first things he'd noticed about her. But that was a hundred years ago and he was bald and paunchy and trying not to take sugar in his tea and cut down on coffee and he'd stopped smoking. Sometimes she felt lop-sided and other times she didn't. If they'd had children she at least would have had them to worry about, but that opportunity had gone by with a few others. There was no real way of apportioning blame, he was always busy and she didn't really enjoy him touching her any longer. He could easily lose a few pounds and take more time off, but neither seemed about to happen. She wore a light dress with only a pair of sensible yellow panties under it and she enjoyed having bare legs and anyway it was hot. The air was full of old heat and it seemed to come out of the gravel and down from the air.

He came back in from the garden, his shadow round on the trimmed grass, bumpy, as if he were made of lumps, and he belched discreetly and smiled at her. *This will do fine*, he said, and he touched the end of her nose with his finger. His teeth were brown and he looked old, she thought.

He looked like an old man and she was in charge of him, but she felt humbled by another quick flare of dizziness and she lat back against the kitchen counter. You should lie down, he said. *I'm fine*, she said. This is par for the course.

The house had a sign on it which read Karreg burned into a wooden plaque that looked as if it had been hived from a living tree. They'd found it on the Web, or she had found it one night when he was working late and she had dragged herself, in real pain back then, to the computer. She'd surfed a hundred different locations and realised that she was having a separate dream about each one as a place to run away to if she found that he was having an affair with a younger woman, someone typically at his office, and

161

she was on her own. If he had a heart attack and she was left on her own that would have some dignity and legitimacy about it, but if he took himself off because of the way she looked now she couldn't stand it. She'd have to move too. Somewhere warm. Then she'd found this cottage in Brittany, a place she knew nothing about and that suited her, she'd have to make discoveries and the last one she'd made had turned her into a disfigured old woman, so what could be worse. She had never liked surprises. Surprises, her mother had told her when she was a girl, always bring their own weight. So she knew that a surprise could mean a death in the family but never a win on the Lottery. He had taken one look at the cottage printed out when he came home very late and nodded and the following day she'd booked it. Two weeks. Then they'd taken her into hospital and given her the first doses, sickened her, taken her mind off cottages in quaint hills. Better than losing it completely, the specialist had quipped, a slim man with neat grey hair and designer spectacles.

He went out and locked the car as if there really were enemies waiting to steal it lurking behind every hedge, though there was nothing but a blue fading valley and hills and some wind turbines white as crucifixes wheeling in the distance. When he came back in he took a fit of coughing and growled about the pollen-count. She sat outside on the steps of the cottage and looked as far as was possible through the gathering mist a few kilometres towards the wind-turbines thinking of nothing. The wine mellowed her, she wanted to doze, but he was making tin noises in the kitchen and then he was cooking something. *We've enough for, well, I don't know what we have enough for*, he said. She looked down and saw that she wasn't as lop-sided as she had imagined and then looked at her waist and felt a small spurt of joy at nothing at all. Things buzzed past her head. She was glad to be here, nicely fatigued after the run from the ferry. She hated being cooped up on anything, a plane or a ferry, but she would have hated even more spending a wet summer at home listening to the drugs dripping inside her like some weird mechanism of an exotic clock. He came out with a couple of sausages, some ketchup and bread-and-butter, he'd brought things from home as if they were in danger of being stranded and starving in a desert waste. She ate and let the melting butter slip around her lips and chin. She thought that in a couple of years she would be the same age as a rock star she'd thought was cool when she was a girl, that is she would be crossing the line like him, entering a hollow epoque when other people told her to act her age, women like herself with sons and daughters who never rang, wrote or visited and who floated in a rancid odour of mouldering wax under Givenchy perfume. She looked like a girl, men looked at her, or had done at any rate. But she still had breasts, just not as much of them. It was all very tedious growing older. Well, one didn't actually grow, one decreased in size. Language bent and refurbished to conceal the obvious. His business was going through a rough patch because no one had spare cash any longer to buy new cars, yet he attended expensive seminars with fools telling him how to grow his business. How she despised the ordinary lies. Maybe he would catch his business in time. Maybe she'd caught what she'd caught in time. Maybe everybody lied about everything.

He refilled her glass and took her plate away and she heard him running water. I'll have a bath, I think, he said. She could smell him from the steps, where he had stood behind and beside her. She could smell his sweat, the gentlest twist of urine. She realised that if a man was coming up the gravel drive he would be able to see straight up her skirt. In a while it was time to take another pill, or maybe it was two this time around, and she went back into the cooling house and heard birds in the eaves get excited and rampant and then a moon came up, a sliver of skin on the hills. He played around with the TV channel-changer and grumbled that it was impossible to get an English-speaking station. They exchanged the kind of banter that came to them without thinking about it or organising it and which meant nothing but filled a space. When the light went down and grey in the front room and the moon rose and got brighter he lit a white candle and placed it on the table, the table was covered in a neat and knitted cloth and there were milk-maids on it, as there were milk-maids in blue on the cups and saucers and even on a milk-jug; there was a very old brown photograph hanging on the wall behind the TV and the figure in it was as insubstantial as a ghost.

The candlelight soothed her, she'd taken her medication and that marked a line in her day. He made as if to sit beside her, that is he came over to where she had sat back on the small settee and it appeared for a moment or two that he'd sit down beside her but he didn't in the end. The hesitation in him hung in the grey air. There was the looming sound of an aircraft very high up and when she leaned back she could see the bright white streak against the dark blue now drawing itself out like a thread in water moving so far and distant and fast that it was unimaginable.

They went to bed together, he leaned over and blew out the candle, she wondered why he'd gone through the business of even lighting it. When the room went dark it seemed brighter outside. She lay on her side while he read a book. When she turned over it was obvious, the half-breast she'd been left with on that side. The room smelled of new wood and deodorant. All the small toiletries in the bathroom had their labels in French. Only by the rough crumpling and crackling did she know he was reading a newspaper and not a book. He said into the room, we're not far from a fair-sized town. She thought, if I had had a son when I'd wanted to, he'd be nearly thirty by now.

It was hot and sunny in the morning and he brought her a light breakfast, trying to make it different, foreign, exotic and simple with what he called *real coffee*, out to a small wrought-iron table just before the gravel started. Her skin tingled in the thick sun poured over it and her chair was uneven on its metal legs. The bread tasted new and raw and she spread butter over it thinking it's creamier than what we get back home, and he poured several thick spoons of sugar into his coffee and kissed her on the cheek. She wanted to take all her clothes off and spread her legs and be fucked by the sun. There was that kind of free and vulgar feeling in the air, and the air hummed and slicked and clicked with insects flying around and the hedges and trees were full of birds. If we put our minds to it, he said, squinting his eyes and cleaning the plastic lenses of his sunglasses, we could have a place like this and retire here. She squinted up at him. He hadn't shaved yet. He looked raw and she felt now would be a good time to stroke one another, to lie together. *Let's find a tourist office*, he said. He slurped his coffee and in the hazy distance the thin blades of the wind turbines began to turn. She went back inside and had a shower, washing all that sun off her skin.

166

The dressing was thin and she pulled it off. The scar was diminishing. The pain when she raised her arm was in a tendon, a nerve, a muscle. Her heart was beating hard just to look at the scar. What was taken out might just have moved somewhere else, gone on holiday in a little house in her lungs or somewhere. But they'd said all the right things to keep her soothed and reasonable. It seemed you could cure anything if you caught it in time. She washed between her legs, felt the firmness of her thighs and the pliancy of herself down there and dried herself down, applied another thin dressing, touched herself up with this and that, smelling suddenly just like she did at home, not as if she were somewhere new at all. Then she took her morning medication and washed it down with water from the tap and said it won't kill me to herself.

He was wearing knee-length shorts designed to make him look like a hunter with pockets for heavy cartridges and quinine, she supposed, and that sort of thing, but they drooped under his belly. He had sandals on brand-new, expensive, with socks. His chest was hairy and full under his flopping Lacoste. He was a postcard, a caricature, her husband, standing on the hot gravel and telling her watch where you put your hands, the metal on the car is roasting. When she opened the car door a small furnace of choking hot air rushed out at her. She was wearing comfortable jeans that outlined her figure and a vest and cotton top with the word GirlWorld embroidered in small blue letters over her cut-in-half breast. They'll look at the word, she told herself, and won't know what's under it. And that made her girlishly smug. *Let me drive*, she said. *Go ahead*, he said, and they climbed over one another, a struggle, hard to do, awkward, and where his penis hid in his shorts passed in front of her face by a few inches. She could have taken a bite out of it.

She adjusted the driver's seat, started the engine. *Drive on the right*, he said, but it was only partly a joke, the rest was his anxiety that she was driving at all. He was always like that, didn't trust her not to kill them both, every time she sat in. She smiled at him and said she knew what she was doing, as she always said, as she'd said on the drive from the ferry and before. He looked out of the window. He liked to drive. He liked to be a man behind the engine of a car. Sometimes they really fought over it. Then sometimes he didn't care.

She drove down the drive and the gravel coughed hotly under the hot tyres. The sun was even hotter through the car windows. Rows of green and dusted hedges gathered speed either side of her. There was a thin puffy white line in the sky where a jet plane passed over. She lowered the window and came to the end of the drive and then there was the tarmacked black road with its mirages of heat like wet glass. *Try that way*, he said, and she pulled on to the left of the road and started driving. She felt big and growing. The sun was on her skin like a kiss after sex. She felt young.

They drove by enormous fields of sunflowers with their faces turned skywards, yellow and open. *We should stop and I'll take a picture*, he said. She pulled over and he got out and spent time being complicated about taking the photo. There were cream-skinned cows low and fat in the fields behind them. Then he got back into the car and she felt his weight in the vehicle. They drove on, she was so careful her neck was tense and there was pain over her eyes. Give me my sunglasses from the pocket, she asked him, and he handed her very black sunglasses, a cheap pair, and she put them on. The world went dark. Even the sunflowers lost their colour. She took them off. The fields moved outwards from the road either side and changed colour from yellow to green and climbed up small inclines and got lost in themselves. There were insect and bird sounds through the open window and now and then the sound of cattle that she couldn't see. There was a river brown and shiny like varnish running along the road now and passing under a sandstone bridge that looked very old, and under a broken wooden mill wheel beside a stone building of two or three floors and there were some cars parked there and a family sitting around a plastic white table with a dubious parasol advertising Pernod. The children's yelps were hot on her face. The road looked black and melting like a strip of liquorice in a child's hand. There was a signpost that said Église Protestante. It pointed up a dry lane. Then it disappeared. Watch your speed, he said. She resented that. She pushed her foot down just a touch, a feather's weight, on the pedal. He looked away, though he must have heard the change in the engine.

He looked away and she drove on and now and then a vehicle would flick past in the opposite direction and once there was a tractor, bigger than she'd imagined a tractor should be, pulsing with gigantic wheels at a dictator's pace. She could hear the car tyres licking the tarmac. She opened and closed her legs quickly and took in some wayward draft of cool air on her thighs. I must send postcards, she thought; then she thought no, or she'd make them cheap ones. A high stone cross, the Christ weathered and melted back into stone, ran by. Or find some gifts, there must be gift-shops, but then she said no, reminding herself that she despised tourist trinketry. There was a bird hovering high in the blue air and she took her eyes off the road and looked at it and he said Keep your eyes on the road, dear. He used to call her honey and now he called her dear. She tried to turn on the radio and he said I'll do that and a roar of French language came out of every station and he turned it off and said It's all in French. There were yellow fields shaved close as if a giant barber had run an electric trimmer over them. They gave off a solid shock of yolk-yellow. There were other fields deep green like sea-pools. Now and then a telephone pole was bandaged in bright posters advertising something but all she caught was a number or a day in black ink, an isolated jeudi or samedi. The posters teased her. Some of them were in a language that wasn't even French, Breton maybe, like Irish but not the same, like Welsh, she'd read, it was still spoken here in some places.

Her hands were sticky on the steering-wheel and the air was cooling under her skirt. The sticky back of the dressing tugged a little at her skin as she moved her arm, so long as the wound didn't weep there was nothing to be concerned about. It could be worse, chemotherapy, a couple of days recovering, a hospital bed where you couldn't sleep and hospital heat thick as old men's breath and a stink of decay everywhere even under the sprays and disinfectants. He would rub his hands in clear antiseptic gel from a wall dispenser every time he was leaving her and it looked like he had to do it just to be in the same room, or that's what it looked like to her, being vulnerable and weepy.

Maybe they'd both entered that age where you got used to hospitals and young people prodding at you with cold instruments and talking in codes. Maybe this was the time of no respect and no privacy and opening your legs and showing your breasts to a kid who could be your grandchild, you had to feel time passing like that, brutalised and unconcerned. Dispassionate and

171

ugly. One time when a young doctor had examined her she had been overwhelmed, shamed even, by the urge to put his hand on her good breast and tell him to feel it properly, tweak the nipple, make her sigh, do it like a man with a woman. She turned a corner and there were two girls cycling, young, their legs in jeans pumping up and down and they were chatting away, one behind the other as the car went by. One had hair dyed blazing red and in the rear-view mirror it looked like the girl's head was trailing blood. If you feel odd or dizzy tell me, he said. Don't brave it out. No I won't brave it out, she said back to him. She turned a sharp corner and enormous vehicles, things from another world, banged by on a slick hot highway several lanes across and she could just make out the word *Entreposage* painted in black lettering high on the rear of a container vehicle higher than a small house. Then the road she was on righted itself and the highway disappeared behind burned brown hedges and only the sounds, growing fainter, remained. *They're going for the ferry*, he explained. Or maybe in the other direction, God knows, Marseille, for all you know. Italy, even.

There were white-walled cottages with thick red flowers in painted boxes on the ledges of their small windows, immaculate, bright, like a child's toy. There was a winking lake through the bushes and trees, like mercury spilled out on a green flowery cloth. The village announced itself with a squat sign and a coat of

172

arms and they were there, a main street with shuttered-up shopfronts, posters advertising circuses and rock concerts leprosying every white flaking space, it was at first like a village an army had deserted. There was a post office with an enormous bronze bull on a plinth in front of it and an ancient spired church. Elderly men and woman moved about very slowly. The corners were chatty tabacs and small bars, she could look inside and see the beery cool twilight and men leaning against the bar and some reading newspapers and stickers advertising lotteries all over the windows. A newspaper headline announced a local bicycle race and the word Sarkozy. There were postcards on turning stalls. You could sit in there all day and no one would ask what you were doing. Maybe he was thinking the same. *Park anywhere you can*, he said, but there was a market in the main square and canopied stalls everywhere and the sound of a generator and no room, so she circled, lost them both, lost the village, found it again, parked under a whistling enormous tree in a spot designated for the use of disabled drivers and he didn't say a word.

*I'm disabled*, she said. *I've only got one tit.*

*One and a half*, he said.

There were shoe-shops, a hairdressers and two auctioneers with windows full of bright photos of local houses for sale just behind where they'd parked and they did what was normal and stared at the photos and admired or disdained the prices. There was a dream sitting in a frame in the windows. Then there was an elderly man in a grey zip-up jacket and a cap, maybe his daughter saw to it he didn't go out like a tramp, kept him neat, and he was sitting on a bench under a high flagpole with a French flag flicking from the top and he was feeding pigeons with chips of crusts of bread and there was no expression on his face doing it. Smaller birds were walking all over his hands, he looked like Saint Francis of Assisi in some sort of painting, all memories of living the good life and repenting later.

There were people coming and going to the stalls in the market and they both felt safe. There were children at the roundabouts and one sharpshooter was firing an air-rifle at balloons and killing them all, every one, candy-floss kiosks and second-hand clothing racks and elegant small women pulling dogs. And here was a café with little red-topped tables outside it and a menu that advertised English Spoken, he was going there he told her, she could browse the market. She went off in among the stalls and he didn't bother to watch her go or see the way the wind made her skirt dress her girlish figure, none of that. Even if he'd looked he wouldn't have seen that. At a window over the tables in the street were two plastery wooden dolls almost life-sized, one dressed as a chef and the other as a girl handing him flowers and the cafe was called Le Blaireau. He thought about walking a few dozen yards down the square to a shop that sold newspapers and buying one just for show, he wouldn't be able to read it. But he didn't want anyone to think he was a paedophile sitting there in his shorts and all those kids playing around. Thankfully, he told himself, you didn't bring a camera, a shot of the market would be nice but you can't photograph anything these days with kids in it. He sat down and a good-looking woman, in her forties but well-breasted and slim, came out of the darkness of the cafe and asked him in English with a thick English accent if he'd like something. He looked at the redness of her throat and he smelled her perfume. That little hidden extra of sweat.

*Do you want to see a menu?*

*No*, he said.

*On holidays?* She said.

So it went. He felt her absence when she left, off to get him a beer. Suddenly there was an English voice, a man's voice, addressing him. A middle-aged man in a straw hat, slightly drunk, was standing over him carrying a packet of cigarettes in one hand and a small cigar in another. *Fucking heat*, he said, and sat down, showing a small stain on his creamy slacks. It was one of those tipsy introductions and he felt awkward for a while then went with it and didn't know where his wife was, the perfume of the café woman was still in his nostrils. The beer came, golden and cold and with a white froth but not quite up to the top of the glass

175

like you'd expect at home. *I saw you looking*, said the Englishman. *Untouchable*, he added. *Her husband's a local.* He tapped the side of his nose. *I've tried.* The Englishman had a small black spot on his cheek and it was hard not to wonder where that small spot had migrated to. Some other foreign village, he thought, down around the liver. We could all have God knows what eating at us. She was lucky she didn't loose the whole tit, for that matter. The Englishman took off his hat and suddenly there were the words of a Noël Coward song, maybe it was Coward, fluttering behind his eyes. *You on holleedays here?* the Englishman asked him, with a frown, which might have been the sun. *Yes,* he said. He seemed to be saying that a lot. *From where? Ireland,* he elaborated. *I went there once,* said the Englishman, and he left it at that and looked away up towards the market stalls.

They were talking and other people joined them and although he had just turned up it seemed they'd been waiting for him for years, they were around him and dragging up chairs, half a dozen by the finish, plump Englishwomen and a couple of sweating men, one of them showing on his chest a zipper where his open-heart job had been sewn up. I won't have anything said about Pakistanis or any other illegal immigrants, the heart man said, because when I opened my eyes after they'd got through with me first thing I seen was a black face under a turban and a

176

smile like a happy arse and he was the doctor looked after me and did a good job, he did. Everyone drank beer and smoked and it was *what I wouldn't give for a jug of Taunton's best*, or *I always drive up to Morlaix, do you know where that is? Well, they have an English shop there, canned stuff like at home, and even copies of the Daily Mirror and Heinz Ketchup. Tea,* said the zipper chest. *Tea too,* said a woman, *Lipton's. Can't beat tea that comes from England, I say. I buy all my house-paint back in Dorset,* a man said, *because the French don't know anything about making good paint, can't get it here. Can't get Sky channel either. Some can. We can't. Five years living here and we still can't get it. When I say living here....*

He meant that he went home every six months, the house would have to be sold or they would have to leave here, couldn't keep two places, that would be a bit much. *The Euro rate's the problem. I went back to get this done,* said the man with the open-hearted scar. *Don't trust Frog medicine, me. Different ways of doing things here and you pay for everything. Don't know what they're putting in or taking out.*

Everyone laughed. He was tired, he'd had more beers than he'd intended and he could see his wife coming across from the stalls, or some direction she hadn't left by, and he felt suddenly embarrassed and guilty. She looked very young in the afternoon sunlight. I'm going to sleep in the car, he thought. He looked at her and she looked at him and smiled diplomatically, though he knew she'd be daunted by a sudden entrance into this chicken-gaggle. *Who's this lovely young lady?* said the Englishman who'd been first to join him. He looked his wife up and down. One of the women around the table was so obese that she exuded a potent animal odour. *You can sit on my knee, love!*

*This is my wife*, he said, and gallantly he got to his feet. He couldn't get it out of his head that these people must have been really lonely to focus on him. *From Ireland, are you?* someone else had asked, and he'd find it shy saying yes, he was. Names were given out around the table and he felt as if he was about to get sick. Hunger or terror. He sat down and swallowed deep on his new beer and felt better. He was nervous for her sake, he didn't know why, she handled herself admirably, put her bags to one side, *I've bought you a shirt,* she said to him. *Lovely things up there and nothing expensive. We must get back and eat,* he said. *I'm not at home now,* his wife said, *I'm not cooking. Well said, my hinny!* someone offered. People laughed. There was rough conversation about who did what and why they were all where they were, the kind of chat that goes on in a bar on a ship at sea when the engines have failed, it had no direction. You could hear the engineers labouring far down below everything trying to keep it moving, inch by sweating inch. He was on holiday, his wife was on holiday, the others seemed stranded there, too long trying to make it work, they'd bought houses, taken up nature painting, tried to brew-your-own but French laws got in the way. Great bloody place if it wasn't in France, one woman said, and she belched and said pardon. He looked at the woman and thought she was going to cry. *Vodka I should have asked for,* she said to no one. *It's not France, my love,* said the Englishman who had brought Noël Coward's song to mind. *France is over there*. He laughed and it was as if he was choking on his own blood.

He could no longer distinguish the men's voices from the women's voices, they were blending together traitorously and they were all annoying him and the light from the yellow pavement was hard on his eyes and he was starting to feel his age, the bakery was closing and shutters were scuttering down and being locked and here and there stalls were being dismantled and vans of all sorts had come in to the square and there was a lot of loading going on. A couple of elderly women with dogs on leads and wrapped tight in thick clothes gabbled loudly on a corner.

Flowers rocked in their vases when a tender breeze soothed the heat. The beers looked flat in their frothy glasses. He put his right hand over his heart as if he was pledging allegiance to something or swearing himself in but he was remembering what his doctor had said about booze and rich food and that his cholesterol numbers were high and took a tiny fright to think what might happen if he keeled over right here in this foreign place and he slugged his beer to dissolve it.

Everyone was standing, the café's hostess came out, there was the usual embarrassing scrabble over who'd pay, he found it schoolboyish and gave up quickly. He saw that his wife was talking to one of the women. They were laughing at something and he thought that was good, a positive sign. Come back this evening, someone said, but it may not have been directed at him. He nodded absently. The man who'd been first to sit with him took his arm and said *there's a good pub, English beer and a big telly all one side of the wall, they get the sports channels from home, brilliant. Owner and his wife's mates of mine. Wife's a bit, you know, nose-in-the-air sort of thing, but he's a Scotsman. Different type. Tits in the air too, if you get me.*

When they'd gone, she looked at him and said it was getting chilly. *Do we have to drive back or will we eat here?* he asked her. *I could do with a cardigan round my shoulders,* she said. *Which is it,* he said. *Eat here, I suppose, if we're meeting them later,* she said. She didn't care. Then he said, *I've had a fair bit to drink. I'll drive later,* she said. *Don't hear you complaining now, do I?* He put his arm around her, the beer was doing that to him. He looked in through the window of Le Blaireau at the comely owner and saw how uprightly and tight she walked, like a woman who

180

knows men are watching, he thought. I would, he thought, I'd take it if it was going. He walked away with his arm over his wife's shoulder and a furtive, almost ridiculous erection squeaked in his holiday shorts. They walked up the square and she went away from him and took a photograph, pulling her camera out of some bag, of the buildings that had plaster and wood fronts and modern shops beneath. A young man and a girl were in a shuttered doorway, the girl playing a fiddle and the young man a tin-whistle and the music attracted her and she went over and threw some coins into a hat. The music was fast and lively and young. Shouldn't encourage them, he said.

She smiled at the young man's nod. That's what I should have been, she told herself, I should have played a fiddle and travelled over the world with a young tin-whistle player and taken drugs and had an abortion or two, would have straightened me out, made me real, as the kids say these days, I should've started fucking ten years earlier. I should never have married him, my husband. But I didn't think like that back then, I thought there was a plan.

She went into a gift shop full of scents of personal and room perfume and she bought scented candles and left him standing outside, didn't know what to do with himself and he squinted in the sharp sunlight. When she came out he was smoking a cigarette. She'd tested some perfume on her wrists and she held them up to him so he could smell it. He looked at her, disappointed.

Standing outside waiting for her he'd looked all the way down the street and noticed the fading lettering on the sides of old buildings, this and that, something advertising beer, one half of a man's smiling face, like a street after a bombardment. He thought to himself that it was as if there was a town under the village or alongside the village and maybe in some parallel universe there was a man, the precise replica of himself, standing on a corner looking left as he looked right, and so forth. There were hills down there and the big highway and lots of distance. He could drive all the way to Italy, or China, for that matter. Once you got off that damned island you could go anywhere, it was the island that hemmed you in. He squinted one eye and the phone wires over the street bent and kinked in the middle. I'm going blind, he thought, that's a sign. I've read about it. When she came out of the shop he knew she'd bought things, candles, and she made him sniff her wrists, a high peppery odour of perfume. The top of her dress opened and he could see her breasts and the bandage, the sticky thing. He remembered what the nipple of the wounded breast had felt like in his mouth, he would bite it gently, the sort of thing you did when you were young and never did again. Biting your wife's breast.

They went into a pizza restaurant that was full of families all talking loudly and children getting down from chairs and slapping one another and happy chaos. There were fake old drawings of Breton women in their flounces and head-dresses, bigouden from another day on the walls and maps and posters for festivals and dances and what was on in the local cinema. A pretty plump waitress came over and smiled them the menu. She had black hair and a round face and could have been fourteen or forty. Efficient, right to the point. *Will I have wine*, she asked herself, she didn't ask him. *Yes,* he said, *do, go ahead, go mad. I don't want to go mad,* she said, and looked at the menu. He didn't know what to say to that, he settled on a big pizza with anchovies, though he didn't know it was anchovies because he didn't know the French word, but he was being daring, enjoying himself, making his food a mystery. He knew his cheese. He made a thing about what sort of cheese was on the pizzas. They drank Breton cider in small handleless earthen cups. They ordered and had a bottle of wine, though it cost them it wasn't as much as they'd imagined, it was red and tasted plump and fruity and decent and when he'd tasted a pinch of it, the waitress offering him just a sip, he poured for her and she let him, hearing the nippy slosh of the liquid round the glass. When he filled his own glass and the girl was gone he felt better and held his glass up in a toast over the table that had a white cloth on it with intricate lace-work on the edges and she lifted her glass and the

183

two glasses clanked over the table and dropped some red drips on to the white cloth. Bread came in a basket, rough and brown and heavy and a lighter white bread, crispy and hard and blonde crusts. They ate without butter. They sipped the wine. *I got you a shirt,* she said, and opened one of her bags right there and then and he saw growing from it a bright red shirt with short sleeves and a button-free collar. *Problem always is the width of my neck,* he said. *I have my grandfather's thick neck, like a bull. You skip a generation.* He looked at it and she held it out but he made no attempt to take it. She put it back in the bag. *It'll fit,* she said. *It'll suit you.*

The pizzas came with salad and were hot and not too heavy, with cheese and anchovies, he was surprised to find out, and she had mushrooms and scooped some up and tossed them on his pizza and he shared his anchovies. They ate and drank and talked about everything and nothing and she watched the children running around and as they drank more it was as if now and then the tables around them were speaking bits, whole sentences, in English. As if the conversations had attained a note which the world could hear and understand, all barriers down. You could almost interject your own comments, you began to know what everyone was talking about. He went to the bathroom and found that yet again it took him a long time to piss and when he did it wasn't up to

184

much, but that was like his eyes, it came with age and it was what it was. The wine had fortified him, truly.

What she noticed was how the various brightly-coloured flavours hung on her tongue, moved around her palate, foreign to her not so much because she hadn't eaten a pizza before, she had and many times, but because there was something other and more about eating it here, the oil dribble golden and more exotically over it, the mushrooms were more succulent and the base crisper and tasting of real flour. The place she was in, she could eat it, take it into herself like a communion host, absorb it. Here was flour that had come from growing in a field of yellow and out of earth that had nothing to do with her. Herbs too that had came from a garden, a field, whose weight of sun she could not imagine but at the same time could only imagine, and the wine tasted like grapes of blood. She took in the difference of where she was through her mouth and nostrils. He'd look up now and then and he'd look at her and his teeth, grey and well-brushed, would fold down over the fragile flesh of an anchovy. Eating is sex, she thought, and she giggled, because the imagery was crude and salty, the idea was crude and salty, and its surprised her because she could never have come up with that back home under the greeny rain. No, this belonged here, this thinking wide of herself, this flighty conjuration. As they left the restaurant, paying by Visa card the smiling waitress and saying as little as possible to her, they strolled along a street of empty shop fronts and sad doors. Posters advertising everything and nothing, hung and fluttered from walls and poles, a local discotheque, a fest-noz, which he took to mean by the illustrations accompanying it, a sort of street festival, and a book sale and other things, and he read everything by symbol and image as if he had never been able to read letters and words. They strolled over a small stone Roman bridge and heard fat toads barracking in the damp grass. The wind came up and it grew heavy and the sun went in and out behind obese clouds. There was a gallery window with a plaster-cast of a human backside in the window, alone, like something blown there by a bomb, there was a note in English on the door saying the sculptor was on holidays but inquiries could be made to an e-mail address. He looked at it and said I wonder if it's the sculptor's ass, and she grinned at him and said nothing because she could see herself reflected in the glass window and her face had become one with the plaster backside behind the glass. They wandered now, the town deserted as if a play had just ended, a piece of theatre just for them, they struggled, sometimes holding hands but they didn't know why or didn't feel the impulsiveness of it, one way or another they moved back up towards where the market had been and a church bell banged out and when they reached the square again they were both winded and tired and it wasn't like a holiday, all this effort.

They sat on a bench beneath the town hall with its cock for a weather-vane and the statue of fallen war dead, so many, and he dozed off and she nudged him in the ribs, people could be looking at them, the police could come and take him away, anything could happen, but when he shut his eyes she felt alone and lost. She stood up and he stood up with her, lighted a cigarette and remembered the name of the bar the Englishman had mentioned. It wasn't far, nothing was far here, and they found it by the thudding noise of music turned up far too loud, disgracefully loud, she wouldn't stand for it if she was living here. There it was, down another hill, a steep hill this time with seats of white painted metal outside at a weird angle for sitting at because of the slope, and a couple of young men in shorts sitting there, loud English accents, drinking beer and smoking and one of them wore a Manchester United jersey. Another turned to look at them both, he had the low-eyed scowl of housing estates where nothing ever happened, full of Alsatian dogs roaming about and things got stolen and an ice-cream van jingled round in the afternoon; he had the raw white face of someone on a bad diet and he stared unashamedly into her crotch where the wind took her skirt and she thought I could be his grandmother but he kept staring.

When her eyes adjusted to the brown gloom she

187

saw a family sitting to one side of the room at a table fretful with beer bottles and even at this hour the remains of fat breakfasts, fried eggs and bacon rinds everywhere, and two round children knocking things over and a copy of *The Daily Mirror*. A handwritten sign on the wall said Internet Access Ask at Bar and another over the counter said All-Day English Breakfast. The family rose and left in a loud fog of shouting goodbyes and the buxom woman behind the counter, clingy black skirt, stout legs without tights, fake tan, waved at them all and one of the men leaned over to kiss her cheek and the women laughed as if this was a secret joke. There was a longer hall which might have been called a lounge with soft chairs sprawled all over the floor and a dart board on a wall and figures that were moving around down there, male and dark in the darkness, carried glasses in their hands. She didn't feel comfortable here, there was some sort of sound system in a corner and, God help us, coloured lights were flicking on and off, it took her back a hundred years to when she was young and she could have taken all of this with a leap and a bound. He was at her side, drinks in hand though the pizza had filled her, here she was anyway, sipping a glass of white wine. Out of the shadows emerged one of the Englishmen from outside the café. Then a door clapped open and the women appeared, out of a Ladies that actually had 'Ladies' in English on it, the whole place seemed to be under siege,

Simla for the rainy season, something like that. She had her cheek kissed and they were inside this low-ceilinged room with the coloured lights hopping off ceiling and walls sitting on a soft chair, all the talk was of how great the owners were and there was the owner himself, thin as a plucked stalk, pushing a metal barrel through the room and a French man appeared, young and grease-haired and slapped him on the back, *Ça va?* The barrel was obviously heavy and someone shouted *Need a hand, mate?* And he didn't even look up. The young French man went up to the counter and behind the counter and gave the woman there a hug and a kiss on either cheek and she held him with one hand longer than was necessary. Everyone was watching this. Everyone was watching the bar owner pushing the barrel and the woman who was his wife being handled and handling back.

The darts went plop! and thud! And there was this sort of cheer and that and some whistling and they were all sitting there drinking white wine or red wine or local beer and he'd have English beer, the good stuff, before the end of the month someone said, and it was hot and clammy, the room was like a bad nightclub. The woman came out from behind the counter and carried a drink of some kind in her hand and said *Hello my darlings* to all of them and sat down, her skirt riding up, her thighs spray-tanned too and thick. Her husband flitted by and then struggled in with another barrel, hollow sounds like Cuban steel in the background when he changed the pipes on empties and replaced them with the full. A blond dog walked in, tongue hanging out in the heat, and then disappeared. A colour photo in a newspaper was being dragged under one of the animal's hind legs, and there was a speedy shot of a racing cyclist, all tight jersey and thick thighs and wrap-arounds, being torn in half slowly.

He was looking past his own wife up the skirt of the owner's wife into darkness as if there was nothing there and she looked strangely scooped out between her legs. The young Frenchman sat with them for all of ten seconds and eventually said he was a film student from Lyons. *Louis from Lion*, said the owner's wife. *Louis the lion!* said another woman and the women laughed. *I know the films he's making,* someone said, and there was more lewd laughter, the seats rocked with it and he could smell these women, their sweat and whatever else, he could smell them and he felt guilty and looked at his wife. She was so quiet, so small, beside them. He looked at his wife and thought the French bloke's banging her, banging the poor bastard's wife, she's straight out of Coronation Street or EastEnders and we're not, no we're not.

No, we're not he thought and turning round saw that the front window of the place, a single window that looked too fragile, was a solid wall of white light where the sun was breaking in, splashing its white paint all over the tables, chairs, the bar and the gathering of plates with the fried egg drying on them. *English?* said the young Frenchman. *No, Irish,* he said, and tried to smile. The young Frenchman put up a mock frown, he had one blue eye and one brown eye, and he said *Ouai! Not English. He's a fucking Frog,* said the Englishman who had first sat with him at the café table, it all seemed like a long time ago and slightly scary. He pointed at the younger man with his raised glass. *Croak-croak!* They both laughed. The Englishman was so crass it was funny. It was like watching two boxers laughing at one another before a fight. The Englishman's face was sweating and he cleared his throat suddenly, a sound that made the women look up. He wore a metallic watch the size of a small beer mat. *Talking while you're swallowing,* a woman said. *I can do that no problem* said the bar owner's wife and again that laughter came up like smoke and the young French man had his hand firmly on her knee, her bare knee, made no pretence, gone beyond all that, even as again her husband hauled an empty beer barrel through the dark room. It was hot.

There was the brief humming sound, a single note, the world makes turning out of kilter so that up was down. He wondered what it would be like to have a heart-attack here and who you'd go to, where you'd get help. He felt fragile, as if he was coming down with something. Christ don't let him come over here and sit down and try to be friendly, he thought. I will break down, I will weep. Something will cause me to disintegrate, implode like a TV set. He gulped at his beer. He felt better. He'd lost himself for a moment, gone away, but he was oozing back.

His wife stood up and excused herself, her form visible through the skirt that seemed suddenly to have become thinner and she made her way with her girl's figure that hadn't carried the weight of a child down to the Ladies and when she pushed in the door there was a stench of bottled disinfectant and the far-away hollow hacking of a cistern. The door to the single cubicle had all sorts of things scrawled on it, she didn't believe women did that sort of thing or at least she'd never done anything like it, juvenile schoolgirl's first period level, she thought, a penis, a man's name, always English names. She was wary about sitting down but the seat, black plastic, looked fair enough and there was toilet paper and when she was washing her hands in front of the mirror she felt relieved in some indefinable way that the mirror didn't have a crack in it. There was scented soap in plunger dispensers the colour of bile. It slicked on her hands and the water was scalding hot when she rinsed them off. She looked at her face in the mirror and saw that her eyes were still blue and wide and frank and open which is what he had said had first attracted him to her but all men lie about that, they calculate cock-first and cynically, she hadn't given in for a long time, she'd played him out and then she'd felt like he was on the point of leaving so that made her mind up. He made this funny face as if he'd been shot or stabbed, it's the same expression really, and then dozed in her arms, which is the romantic way of looking at things but in fact he been a weight on her and she was glad when he rolled off and his prick was like a sausage with the meat squeezed out. She opened herself to herself and saw the half-breast when she pulled back the dressing and she thought she looked fine, I look fine, I look able, and she buttoned up again and went back into the gloomy room with its couple of darts players who could have been in Brittany or Bristol for all they knew or cared. She made her way up the room and saw the little knot of plumpy women and their couple of husbands and the young French man and the owner's wife, but now he was standing against the side of the bar with the owner's wife and she was telling him in English, of course, that she had to get back to work and he pushed her and the plates with the drying egg on them rattled and might have fallen off. The women at the table let out a screech, music-hall fun, naughty Brighton postcard canoodling.

She felt a light tingle run through her scar. She could be as bold and brazen as anyone, join in the fun, make a postcard of herself. She stood over them and lifted her dress high, standing there, her dress rising up her still good legs right to her yellow bargain-store panties and her bush hair out each side of the elastic where she had once felt her own husband's mouth gratefully inhaling her as if she were pure, pure air; and then a bit more and her husband stared at her, stared, and the English man seated beside him stared and then the other men and the women, their wives, sweating and their fingers fat with absurd rings stopped laughing and stared at her, moving from her belly to her face to her eyes.

He stood up. He said something but she couldn't hear him. She let her skirt drop down and asked him like a woman leaving a high-class dinner party, *Shall we go?* And it was all theatre, pure spectacle, her heart banging away like it was up against a wall or a bar counter and here he came, taking her by the arm, not wanting to leave or stay, caught like a ghost in mid-air or halfway between heaven and hell, she smiled openly and one of the women, to give her her due, understood something and clapped her little hands together and said quietly *Nice one* almost under her breath. *You're full of surprises,* her husband said, his legs very hairy as they tried to break out from behind the table and the puffy chairs and trying to make a joke of it, keep it light, and *You're on for a good time,* the English man said, the one who'd invaded his bloody space at the café table in the first place, and the women laughed again and she raised her fingers and twinkled a

194

goodbye and said polite as a psychopath *See you again soon* and walked out past the French man and the owner's wife who hadn't seen anything and didn't care, her thighs waddling looking like a map there were so many obvious blue-grey veins. Tacked to the side of the counter under her legs was a poster inviting you to visit the town's spaniel museum.

Out in the warm evening sun of the street she didn't know what to say, didn't know what he'd say, wondered if she done what she'd done because the mixture of medication and booze wasn't a wise one, but he put his arm around her and they were walking up the street and after a while with the odour of alcohol in his words he said *That place is insane. You'd end up mad as the rest of them*. When they got back to the square people were starting to walk about slowly as if they were building up to something and young men phutted by on badly-serviced motorbikes, that sort of typical evening atmosphere, normal and comforting. She wondered who was going to drive now they'd both had something to drink, he'd had more than she had but how strict were they here? She could always plead that they were tourists. He leaned over and whispered in her ear, following his words with his tongue, that if she'd done what she'd just done in the bar in front of him down an empty street he'd have sorted her out like a twenty-year-old. She felt his hot breath in his ear and then it went away and her ear was cold. It didn't matter whether it was true and she didn't believe him but at least he'd said it and they walked around the square a couple of times, a village square somewhere different in the warm air with all sorts of other people and they even bought ice-cream.

# Carnival

'To look at the night that has been beaten to death; to go on shifting for ourselves within it.'

René Char: *On a Night Without Ornament*

Words dropped out of conversations like confetti.

The evening had dissolved into shadowy liquid corners of twos and threes chattering behind coloured lights and music. I moved between the kitchen and the big square room where a DJ with a blue tint to his cropped hair fussed with great theatre over records and jibbered into the microphone. No one listened to him. The music formed a wall of sound. He drank whiskey from a small glass and sweated.

In the kitchen, paper plates waited in stacks and now and then someone lifted one and helped themselves to a cold meat selection or a dip of curries. A young man I did not know, wearing an apron, cleared away soiled plates. A woman's voice sounded in the hallway and every head turned. Her face, quite beautiful, appeared in the kitchen doorway. She was noisily drunk. She announced herself above the raw music.

Just being here carried its own burden of fatigue, as if a hot wind had delivered a gradual cafard. Everyone here knew everyone else. Affairs were discussed; who had jilted who; the usual rumours of illness and inevitable emigration; petty betrayals and crimes governed by the unwritten laws of a protective community in a small rural town. Just to look around the room was to inspect a nervous and speculative soul that had dragged some level of tolerance from growing prosperity and a bought-in sense of culture. There was no one at this party who did not have at least some money. Occasionally someone entered the circle who was broke but had instead some vague sort of talent. There were always clowns, the sad ones who thought that to be loved they had to dress like Marlene Dietrich and dance on tables. They had their drugs in the toilets, or their weeping. There was always, still, something drearily Victorian about the manner in which our huddling society vetted newcomers. In the end, and further echoing that age, it was left to the recognised aged aunt to pass a final verdict.

He was in his early fifties, immaculately dressed by Dublin and London. He owned a gift shop, dealing in quaint and useless knick-knacks of no value from Hungary or Romania, exotically priced. Ashtrays of shell, Edwardian photographs in gold-plated frames, walking-canes with fake silver handles, candles which gave off scents when burned, heart-shaped sweets, and note paper made from pulped cloth, Indian head scarves; he made money because no one was yet quite sophisticated enough to know the difference between taste and vulgarity. He had need of a new wardrobe now and then, and when he went on his trips invariably he took with him someone he would outfit from his favourite shops. He threw parties and introduced strangers. He was liked and respected and it would be hard to know exactly what we'd do without him. Tonight he had found a new lover and had introduced the youth into our society with the hasty nervous exuberance he imagined necessary. We'd been together once. For a long time. We still shy-eyed one another at parties and in certain pubs. He came over looking for my opinion. He had trimmed his greying beard and tidied his hair. His open shirt allowed a solid gold Saint Christopher medallion to quiver and glint in the coloured lights.

'He seems like a nice lad.'

'Yes. He's young. I'll have to be careful with him. Or prudent.'

He looked at me and smiled, his eyes crinkling at the corners in a way that was endearing and yet hinted vaguely at the amorous savagery behind the elegant nervousness. Each time I saw him I knew why we had been lovers and how. I did not regret him and often wondered whether he regretted me. It was one of those quizzical memories that never quite dissolves with time. I had been young with him. He had been somewhat less successful. There hadn't been much social activity then; there hadn't been so much caution, there was a sort of social timidity. He had risen above all of this and become a mentor. He had placed in local newspapers tiny and barely-tolerated advertisements announcing his monthly parties and giving, bravely back then, his telephone number. He had conquered a tiny empire of shadows.

'You're looking tired,' he told me. 'Are you taking care of yourself?'

'Yes, I think so,' I said, trying to avoid his eyes.

'How old, now? Hitting forty? More?'

'Forty-three, actually.'

'Come and see me,' he said, lowering his voice. 'Old friends are best. Promise?'

He raised a finger of his right hand and stroked my shoulder. It was a light touch, as if a butterfly had attempted to land there and faltered, its wings hammering the air. An electric shiver coursed the bone and buried itself at the base of my neck. I swallowed.

'I'll refill that drink,' he said.

I looked beyond him, to profane memories that were still sacred. I saw the youth dancing with the drunk woman in the middle of the floor. Inexplicably, and only by an authority granted by the mentor himself, the DJ had been forced to play a recording of the Concerto De

Aranjuez by Rodrigo. The Allegro of the First Movement drove their awkward dance. Hands clapped. The lights twitched and throbbed. The woman's pleated skirt circled outwards and hovered like a small tent over the coloured floor. The youth swivelled and his thin toreador hips vanished in half tones of light. The performance fed the woman's need for attention and the young man's desire for acceptance.

'No,' I said, surprised at my firmness. 'In fact, do you know, I think I'll go.'

'This is ridiculous. You've seen me with other men before.'

He didn't understand. Neither did I, I suppose. The music twisted outwards from the dancing room and, now and then, the DJ, frozen in blinks of light, glanced in our direction as if waiting for a signal to stop everything, to return to the anonymity of music which created decent vacuums. He looked over my shoulders, two picador stabs of his eyes. A paper plate flapped helplessly from the stacked pile. The hand-clapping continued. A voice came up from the stair well reciting poetry in Irish:

> 'D'aithe na bhfileadh n'uasal,
> triaghsan timheal an tsaoghail

Two middle-aged men in dark suits looked at us and stopped talking. They disappeared into the roomful of

Rodrigo, and, above the litany of noise, a line broke free in the Irish tongue, its deadening natural poetry brutalising the careful execution of a Spanish guitar and an orchestra of finely-tuned strings. But, for me, the greater poetry of the evening already lay in its graduation into tragedy.

'If it's the music...'

'No, music's fine.'

'Madrigals. I remember you had a fondness for them. Dove, dove e la fede, Che tanto mi giuravi... Do you remember that one? Rinuccini.'

His voice was too weighted for singing and always had been. But he brought the words back to me, a stinging memento, new and frosted with the poisonous sweetness of evenings of love, when other people had not been so necessary. I wanted to hurt him and free myself and I smiled.

'Where was your faithfulness, when it was needed?'

He lowered his eyes. The delicate lashes stung me again and again. I had to get away from him, out of their reach. The swelling music of Rodrigo and the flashing youth and the woman whose laughter now destroyed even the spasmodic poetry of the Irish language. The room drifted free of the music and lights and I saw it as it would be later, when the crowd had gone weary into the wet breath of the morning, and he and the youth were alone, one embarrassed, the other uncertain. A sofa would fold down to make a bed, the lights would be extinguished one by one, and their children's giggles would become frail whispers beneath thin veils of cigarette smoke. Rain would come in from the sea and spray the single square window with salt flicks of its green tongue. The morning would be reborn in the single hard caress, the pup's yelp of pleasure which no ear in the grey streets would detect. The chant of their male struggle would ring within the dim ear of the room and the note would be clearer than Rodrigo or any other music and crucifying. I wanted to forget the future.

'I just want to go,' I said. 'I've enjoyed myself, and thank you.'

'If that's the way, then. Goodnight, Vienna.'

I smiled as Judas must have smiled, feeling his wet lips burn. '*Slán*,' I said, and he moved aside. Rodrigo exploded to a loud halt and there was gunfire applause. He touched my shoulder, anointing me, and I went down the stairs. I heard his big voice silence the beating hands. As another new lover ascended the throne to sit at his right hand, an old one, deposed, scurried quickly out of Gethsemane to hide among the ruins.

A friend of mine once told me that the night streets of any large town are beautiful in the same way a whore is beautiful; I think I understand what he meant. The ugliness has been dressed up, manicured, the subtle cosmetics of lights from shop windows and passing traffic, the winking sluts' eyes of traffic lights, the more delicate fluid sheen of honey-coloured take-away cafés devours the grey tawdry mystery of mercantile daylight. A new town is born, innocent and anxious to acquire the brusque pleasures of rape. The town gets dolled-up to take chances, to tolerate risk. I heard the heavy-painted white door creak and thud behind me and I emerged into the old streets and their new light. The buildings on the main street leaned like old gossips, head to head.

A taxi drew in against the kerb and a beautiful girl dressed in a ballet tutu and pumps laughed out into the air. A young man in a silvery suit and white shoes, a diamond ring in his ear, paid. The girl noticed me, then looked again. She stared at my white dickie tie, a discreet and sacred symbol of my fragile brotherhood. She came over to me and asked, this glowing doll, for directions to the party. I pointed back down the street, not quite knowing what party she meant. She thanked me and giggled off with her young man. I wondered who had initiated her, and if the young man were merely a decoration. She was a girl whose turbulent beauty might be found behind a bank counter or in the fashion section of any women's magazine. I had acknowledged, with one quick glance at her young man, that he hated me and my kind. The taxi moved off. I walked away. Here and there an ancient family crest, carved in grey stone, protruded from a gable wall. A gryphon made ready to leap forward and tongue the gilded night air. A rampant lion, eyes erased by the salt sea-wind, clawed blindly at the town from which his mystery had been born. A mediaeval doorway imposed itself suddenly amidst a clutch of nagging broad shop fronts, the moulded gentle arch elbowing the brutal modern formalities. Over a bank of stone a coat-of-arms announced the passing of tribal years, and hinted that the dragons guarded fundamental secrets. A corner window, lancing over the street, whispered of love-songs ejaculated in the fire of hasty romances, the glass of the windows timid and empty. A newspaper fluttered along the gutter like a woman's dropped handkerchief. A drunk muttered, a coiled black heap, in a doorway. A young man in shirt and jeans slumped over a table in a late café, sprawled among cardboard cups and plastic cartons of anorexic French fries bleeding with ketchup. His little tragedy was framed in a window of plastic wood and roughly-puttied squares of immaculate glass, and the silence around his dead form was brittle as sugar. I walked on, aware that I was on the longest midnight walk of all, and that once begun it could not be interrupted; the choice was my own every time. How many others searched as I did, or would find it necessary to search, before the light of a new sun dissolved us from the streets like sullen vampires? It was a secret, something no one talked about, the unsavoury element dwelling vitally in all of us. Behind the unhurried new respectability lurked this need. Its strength was my weakness and the cruelty most likely to destroy me and baptise me in the final irredeemable humiliation. Young couples giggled by. In the broken phraseology of their laughter I saw the dark quality of my present, as if we had chosen to live in the shadow of death, a generation of suicides. I saw how, as they passed me by in a flick against the wide blazing mouths of shop windows, each gust of their joy exhaled the same frustration and fury which bore me upwards towards the square where the lights and the noises of the world were subdued. And if occasionally I had heard the word Fag drop with its beautiful sister Queer from the rustling trees of adolescent discontent on similar streets, still I had felt the oddly ennobling weight of the words, which described ends of cigarettes and odd things rather than human conditions. They reminded me of lines learned a thousand years ago in yellow classrooms to the panting of confused hearts, where the sweep of my Latin master's dust cloak through the narrow door of our rooms signalled my changing and forming:

*Se iactabant, quasi victores fuissent...*

A line from a poem, an account of battle, a letter. A text-book, perhaps. Its poetry, however unintentionally, had lodged in the shelves of memory. Now and then I found a moment to take it out and dust it over. The young hetero couples on the night streets undoubtedly considered themselves victorious over the world; their easy manner conveyed the brilliance of their naïveté. I knew sad men who had lingered too long in a riot of doubt and become contaminated by an uncertainty that eventually paralysed them. The greatest bravery surely lay in giving up, abandoning oneself to that nature which insisted most strongly. Once the surrender was complete, the midnight trawlings and the unending solitary sweet anguish could begin.

The streets on which I walked were as bright as burnished bronze, with the psychedelic texture of oil on water, as dark as stagnant pools. A rhythm grew up from them, the promise of an illicit harvest, that broke upon the ear like a persistence of rain. It was necessary to respond; I walked, head down and my eyes well turned from the eyes of others, praying that I was in some part invisible. It was difficult not to want to return to the party I had abandoned. But like a good deal of my past, and it might have stood as a symbol for it, the party was now a tiny oasis of hurt enclosed in a manic gaiety and clownish colour. Out in the streets there was at least the invisible carnival to dance to, the thrumming unconscious song that beckoned out of doorways, in a lover's laugh, in the accelerated protest of a passing car and the malicious come-on of traffic lights.

I came to the top of the street and the town square was in front of me. It was blacker than I had known it, and the few dark strutting figures around its gleaming silver cascade of a fountain looked like sentries guarding a sacred idol. Now and then a wind grabbed a spume of water and shook it violently. Some of the figures were sprayed with water; they bent over, twisted around, scattered here and there; always they returned to a kind of absurd order about the fountain. Across the street, humming in sleepy ranks, taxis lined up and seemed to converse in a secret dialogue of open windows and raised bonnets, and the occasional red arc of the tip of a cigarette as it was flicked through the crystal air.

From the window of a cabaret bar on the far side of the square floated the anonymous voice of a singer, the electrified chords of his guitar tinny and unharmonious and his fake Texan drawl limp as soaked newspaper. The sound bore its own weight of sadness, as if the singer sang to save his life. I walked across the pedestrian slabs of white paint and stood on the vast square island that contained a public park, a public lavatory, a pair of ancient cannon pointed at the sealed doors of a bank, and the oracular fountain.

The air murmured with the blood-tang of wet metal and the spice of newly-mown grass. This was a pocket of salvaged green in a sea of thunderous grey concrete. All the distance down its gently-sloped belly to the glowing facade of an enormous cliff of a hotel, the green park seemed to undulate coyly in the damp dark light. I touched my fingers to the cool cement of a lamp-standard, and felt beneath them the lingering and relentless pulse of the town coursing up from the drained, reinforced concrete, veins thick as the height of a man, as if somewhere in the chilled tunnelled murk a great heart pumped and boomed. I stood in the halo of withered neon light and looked nervously at the line of telephone kiosks raggedly illuminated by bare bulbs, and, more directly, with the delicious anxiety of one who is, again, about to commit an abhorrent and revered crime, towards the open mouth of the public lavatories.

Old moments of regret, anticipation, greed and a great deal of impatience. A male figure would burn out of the yellowing shadow of the Gents with the determination of a wooden figure emerging into a tableau on an ornamental clock. There was something abstractly painterly about the way the figure dissolved from yellow into black. It didn't matter that I had carried out this operation before, the inaudible thiefy yell of it seemed once again to carry across the park to the exploding cliff of the hotel, echoing back disfigured and obscene into the self-righteous whoredom of the town's narrow streets. I felt spied upon, knowing I was not. Everything in the next last moments would be left to chance, behind muted sounds, scrabblings, whispers, sleights of the throated word. I had been the discoverer of some ancient dolmen around whose grubby sides a secret language was notched; hidden in its unravelling was the name of our tribal god whose blessing I sought, and in these pounding moments I peered through the candle-flame coloured light for a clue, my squinted eyes like fingers tracing the mutilated rock. I watched for the magic signs – the way a hand was held, a hip bevelled, a head angled to imitate brazenness or nonchalance. The fear of being abandoned here on this threshold, while the secret furled back under the cloak weaved by these fragile priests, always made me turn my head towards the gossipy taxis, plotting a route of escape in the event that I was overcome with embarrassment. I looked, inspected, searched. I let the redeeming wind, full of salt and the semen-smell of the sea, revive me. The sound of far water crashing on stones almost hypnotised me. The lights of the immobile taxis grimaced. The singer's voice crashed out over the square evoking strange agonies. The scent of a passing cigarette soiled the air. A bus, made gigantic and frightening by a faulty exhaust-pipe which permitted it to howl gracelessly, convulsed round a corner and went on with a staggering lean, full of very young faces and throwing off the tattery rags of a scream. I put both hands in the pockets of my trousers. Behind me a drunk announced himself by banging a bottle against a wall and cursing loudly.

A fine mesh of rain threw halos around the street

lamps. The town cowered under the new sudden weather with its memories of drowned galleons and Spanish sailors buried in the Old Cemetery; in the iron bowels of unloading coal boats a sing-song of sweat and commerce was starting up. Out of nowhere, I remembered how I'd been made to remember lines from Molière on evenings darkened by winter rain, the classroom windows fogged by acned breath:

*'Allez chercher vos fous qui vous donnent à rire...'*

Perhaps, had I stayed at the party, I might have found them, those fools. Or perhaps I was just such a fool. The rain made me melancholic. Now the timid priests outside the lavatories raised their bare heads, their moist eyes, to the drizzle; was every time like the first? When at last I had caught his attention, the one I had selected or who had selected me, he was always someone else, the Other One, the one I had not considered.

He wore the faint essence of incense, a memory of whatever hope had forced him in front of a mirror, made him shave, made him put on a new shirt. He possessed a sort of subdued cunning, his smile was vagabond wide. He wore a light talc of embarrassment, but it seemed suddenly false, like make-up dissolving the rain. We pretended, according to ritual, not to notice one another. But at the same time we moved closer, as in a dance whose steps were very old and practised, each of our steps corresponding to the steps of the other. His hair, trimmed neatly behind the ears, sparkled with pearls of rain. His sharp shirt was opened at the collar and he carried a loose denim jacket across his shoulders like a dulling hussar from a tale by Lermentov. We looked one another up and down as best we could in the streaming light. The others squinted to see us, then turned their silent verses round the altar once more in the rain.

I moved off and he followed. I heard his leather footsteps slap in the new puddles. I waited for a car to pass and watched the windowsful of drunk faces watching me, jesters' masks, grotesques; I crossed the street and left the island of the square and its rituals behind me. I stopped and looked into the window of a women's clothes shop. If I looked odd or conspicuous now, what did it matter? The mannequins leered and puckered their lips. Sculptured sex. I saw his reflection take shape in the window and he was behind me, his face pocked with the red flare of a cigarette. The odour of Gitanes carried heavily on the wet street wind. Cars gushed frantically behind him and somewhere in the vastness a woman screamed.

'You like one?'

A young voice, educated. I feared the rough ones, with whom no plea for tenderness ever took root and who knew only the outrage that came with their pleasure and was most of it. He offered the blue packet, crushed in clean, sturdy fingers. I drew out a cigarette and he lit it while I held it in my fingers, closing my eyes to fend off the close flare of the match. The sharp black tobacco burned my throat. He smiled. He was not new to any of this. He knew the moves. He carried his experience, which wiser minds might have interpreted as pain, in the stigmata of thin lines at the corners of his eyes. Our cigarette smoke married in the air, blue and sinewy. We moved away from the eye of the window. Already sticky pools of yellowish vomit slid slowly into the gutters.

'We've really had no summer to speak of,' he said.

I watched him adjust his jacket; his cloak, an Elizabethan gentleman out for a stroll. His accent floated away like a grained melody, a perfunctory madrigal. His eyes, unlike mine, never left the eyes passing us or drew back from their illuminating beam. His fear was my fear, but he had refined it. We were bonded, yet he could not ease my burden of street-deep anxiety. The town's mystery would turn against us in someone's second glance, two policemen looking at us – all they could do was look, of course, their remembered Medusa gaze – a car that slowed down behind us. We walked in a stiff tightening grip, afraid to submit to a cheapening cowardice. So we walked on even more determinedly. Above us, under the black shafts of drainpipes turned glorious and noisy and silvering the rain, a coat-of-arms dripped fretfully, unicorns rampant and sad.

In the mockery of a glass window, a youth wrestled with the arm of a fruit machine and made it screech. The music of a crackling radio jerked out into the street and behind the counter leaned, bored, a beautiful girl whose eyes were black pearls glinting in neon light behind a dead white face. At the open door, the thick smell of burning meat.

'Are you hungry?'

He smiled at me. He was telling me not to pity him, that wasn't in the script, he did not do this for a living like some of the others, he was not a beggar. He was not a prostitute. My shame turned into a smile just like his.

'No, I think I'm fine.'

We walked on. The sounds of the radio dimmed behind us. I turned various things over in my head; I had drink in my flat, cigarettes, a little food, nothing fancy but nothing depressing either. I had what money I had safely locked away. And there was little else of great value there. A sign announcing a Chinese restaurant broke out of the grey monotony of shut facades above us, its cryptic pictographs vibrating in loud red. A faint hiss of oriental music filtered down from the waxy garlanded upstairs windows. Gentle cutlery tinkled. I felt the air begin to dry out and a light warming breeze muttered amongst the discarded newspapers and shattered cardboard cartons sheltering in the gutterings and doorways. The language of disuse, of things tossed aside. Suddenly I felt quite cold and very far removed from the youth who, deep now in the upturned collar of his jacket, had become silent, as if contemplating something private and secret.

A girl ran out of a streetful of noise, her long dress trailing and fluttering like a cone of nervous birds around her slippered feet. The dress was pulled tight at the waist and her blouse was embroidered with thin threads of gold and blue, silver and green. The puffed sleeves were made of a transparent white material. On her head and tied beneath her chin, was a tall conical hat, tapering off into a trailing gossamer scarf that looped and waved behind her as she ran. Behind her, shouting, came a tumbling young man in blue and red striped leotards and green ankle boots. Above his waist he wore a singlet of green and over it flapped the wings of a jerkin of yellow suede. The collar of his singlet was open and the sleeves billowed as he scampered around the corner. The girl piped a laughing scream and disappeared.

The street was suddenly heavy with triangular coloured bunting. The arched windows of shops and houses were flung open and people leaned out, jabbering, into the street. Here and there a knot of young girls, excited and unable to stand still, dressed in flowery skirts and balancing conical hats on their

215

heads, broke out of themselves and pavaned across the street. Young men in coloured hose curtsied and bowed theatrically, waving handkerchiefs. Music flowed down over everything and there was the bone-click of applause and the whine of bagpipes. Stone dragons, enjoying themselves, grinned with broken teeth from forgotten corners. At the end of the street a display of fireworks whirled and exploded into the sky, frightening children in tiny outfits of hose and sequined jackets. From an open-sided lorry a white gash of light framed the figure of a thin man in doublet and hose, with long tapering sleeves and shoes with bells on the curling toes. Beside him a very fat man, purple in the face and with sparse growths of grey hair, dressed in a Tudor outfit of gaudy coloured tunic and ham-coloured tights, and holding what appeared to be a rolled parchment, fidgeted and smiled as if he were in pain while the thinner man fiddled with a microphone. Above them, lapping in the salted breeze, a canvas banner announced eight hundred years of the town's prosperity.

We moved into the street and the lights of windows blessed us with a wafery indulgence. The air was knitted loosely with threads of fabulous scents, or roasting meat, onions, spices, gunpowder, sleepy perfumes. A girl grazed my arm with her capricious pink scarf, filmy as fresh snow and fleeting as a kiss. The young men and girls were notoriously beautiful,

216

laughing in each other's arms, frantic with young joy, drinking from glistening glasses that turned into crystal goblets in the swaying light of a thousand coloured bulbs. Their faces were illuminated by a holy and infectious lust that did not have the crude value of sin. Now and then their faces became transparent and I could look through them to the onlookers who were not taking part in the festival, who were not yet committed to the fantasy. I looked down and expected to see my own clothes transformed, but they stayed the same. Clearly I had not joined in either. The young man who strode along with me, who now and then betrayed his agitation in a grimace as a hand touched against him, began to look lost and vulnerable, like a precious metal losing its sheen. A child dressed in a veiled head-dress and trailing yellow skirt, and whose beauty was the mania of icons, slipped in front of me radiating a small so intense that she made me feel inexplicably tender. A young boy blazed at me with dreadful owl's eyes and pulled his short cloak across his shoulders in a childish challenge. A nattering of bats arced between the conical hats and clicking scarves and whistled back up into the darkening eaves. I felt conspicuous and, oddly, unclean, and that my companion somehow felt the same. He shuddered in an unmistakable gesture of pain. I wanted to be drunk enough to dissolve helplessly and irresponsibly into the colour and noise all around me, swallowed in its glamour. I tapped the young man on the elbow. He looked at me coldly. He was preparing his retreat. I felt a shiver of panic. It was too late, too far to be alone.

'Here.'

He seemed relieved. We huddled in a doorway and I scrabbled for my key. The sexual slide of the key into the lock calmed me. The door opened into a dark flight of stairs and the old odour of extinguished candles. I turned on the light. The wallpaper bloomed with graveyard flowers and the carpet up the stairs had been weathered to a rut. The festival closed out behind us, and a thinner, more sinister cackle broke down upon us from above. I felt my companion treading the stairs behind me, knowing he was inspecting every move and muscle of my body, as I intended him to.

The darkness, suffused with murmurs that seemed to melt out of the mourning walls, dressed us in a mantle. We attained the landing in complete silence. The radio spat sound. A bicycle leaned at a wounded angle against the wall, there was the smell of boiling fat. I unlocked my door and went in before him, sensing him pad behind me like an unnerved animal. The notion of crushed roses hung in the air beyond my threshold. The air in my rooms was still, the hallway suddenly very dark.

Without uttering a sound I turned on the kitchenette lights and indicated the sitting room, such as it was. The game of delicacy, of manners, I suppose, always begins this way. There was no hint of the shared gentle brutality to come. I heard him flop onto the settee. A match struck and I heard him exhale. Through my kitchenette window the tapering banners of the uprights of a ghostly marquee cracked in the breeze off the swollen river and a moon the size of an apple shivered in the gauze sky. Magic drifted over the steep and tiled old roofs. The street had become contaminated with it. I wondered about the party I had left, and to what stage it was now spiralling down. I looked at my face, caught its glass reflection, in the black window. Crow's feet. Eyes whose histories lay etched at the edges in sad ogham. Stories of nights of playful inquisitions and the hurried downfalls of fumbled loves. I saw my face staring back at me, not knowing who I was, a curious stranger at the window. I turned away and seized a bottle of white wine, two glasses, and carried these into the sitting room where he had adjusted the lighting to a brazen table-lamp red. He was standing up now, inspecting my rows of books. He looked around, saw me, returned to the books. He seemed to have taken command in my room, merely by removing his jacket and standing in front of a bookcase. I resented all of a sudden the heaviness of his presence, its complete there-ness. But I was helpless before it, of course. I watched him inspecting the spines of my books and heard the pages rustle and whimper in his fingers. He might have been lecturing a bored Friday afternoon class.

'Incest is always interesting. For example, Victor Hugo hinted strongly in his Notre Dame de Paris that Quasimodo was Esmeralda's spiritual brother. I've always imagined they were more than that. The love he showed her appears quite pure. But read between the lines, the notion is there, all the same. What a well-read little fucker I am!'

Well, there was no answer to that. He replaced the book. The timbre of his voice had altered, the tones assumed colours they had not worn in the street. I recognised a street angel whose wings might take any shape, any size, the level of his flight any degree and reach. It hurt me, strangely, to realise that he expounded on Victor Hugo, or that he could, and found literary theorising interesting, and perhaps considered it part of his service to me, for what it was worth. He ran a slim white finger along the quivering edges of religious and philosophical works. He leafed through another slim volume. The pages fluttered like leaves. I placed the glasses on the side table and wrestled with the cork in the bottle. From the street came other noises, a woman's rising banter, a man's roar, the sound of crushing glass. Above it all, the shrill madness of traditional music. The moon, I knew, looked on.

'"The heart is wiser than the head, and knows more." Do you believe that?'

'It depends,' I said limply. This sort of aphoristic

banter made me feel like a fool. Even if it did inflate his ego. 'Perhaps you'd prefer something else? A whiskey?'

He regarded me as if across a very great distance. He replaced the book with sarcastic attention to finding exactly the right place, and that its spine sat flush with the rest. He did not want me to ignore him. The tiny skirmishes had begun. He knelt at the side table while I poured the colourless wine. I glanced at his face, saw that he was older than he appeared, that he tried hard to take care of himself and his appearance, and that now and then, like all of us, he failed and wore too lightly the great fear that one day no man would look at him twice. He took up his glass, sipped, and winced. In the street, fireworks exploded and sang little arias.

'I could do with some music.'

'Classical music,' I said, 'Is virtually all I have. Not into your Hip-Hop, Garage, Trance or any of the rest of that shit.' I needed to bring him down a little. Not much, just enough. He didn't respond.

'Beethoven, Schubert. The deaf and the emotionally-maimed. Chopin coughing blood on the piano keys. Handel, deaf as a post at the end. I know enough about music. You cannot be a good whore unless you show at least the semblance of an education. Maupassant painted his whores as idiots. They are not idiots. They cannot afford to be. Did you ever pick up a dilly who did not have at least a passing acquaintance with Shakespeare?'

221

'A fucking dilly?'

What an odd, old-fashioned word to use. Were we going to play out some fantasy around Wilde and Piccadilly Circus? He was right. I had never taken much intellectual interest in the young men who haunted the tabernacle at the square. Use-and-discard was written on their foreheads, as perhaps it was written on mine. I had no duty to know them in any such sense, or to understand them. We all carried our burdens of unlocked histories and moral devaluation and the rest; we engaged in transactions, with or without an exchange of cash. We did not, God help us, become friends. Nothing mattered the morning after. But here he was, this educated young man who wanted to describe himself as a Victorian whore, in so doing doubly distancing himself from himself, telling me that none of this was worth much if it didn't at least have its moments of informed discussion. I turned on the CD player.

'Yeh. A dilly. A piece of rent. Read your history. Wall speakers! Flash!'

He'd dropped into a sort of corner-boy street accent. It annoyed me. It mocked me.

'That's enough crap.'

He smiled, I bent over the CDs, deliberately arching my back. I heard wine plop into his glass and applause leap up from the street as if he'd performed a feat of magic and everyone had witnessed it. I heard him take the wine in his mouth and swallow hard. I found Sibelius and flooded the room with the high energy of his Andante Festivo. When I turned back to the settee, he'd sprawled like an arrogant adolescent at my feet, his long legs marking the piled carpet in long shadows.

The Minor chords rose and fell like disturbed flowers in a breeze. The music of Sibelius' own funeral spilled out of the wall speakers like silver water. I tasted the full tart edge of the wine and watched as the music assumed the shape of the room. The movement of the young man's hands around the wine glass or fidgeting over his legs drew out a sustained ballet of rough harmonies. Outside the laughter of every festival in the world jerked, hesitated. I pictured the river in full winterspate charging towards the bay and the Atlantic, giddy with the wreckage of dreams and terraced with drowned bones. I remembered one or two names who had ceased to be names in the dark unwatched glide from the river's bridges through icy air like a rush of diamonds into the blond crests of water, at least one killing illness while killing himself, and in so doing they had become immortalised in the folklore of a small forgetting town. I had often wondered – being careful not to wonder too hard – if any of them had spent evenings laughing over wine and music; or if, because of the way they had chosen to express themselves in death, their lives had necessarily been spent in mourning and anxiety, every day the same. It frightened me to understand, with a poignant clarity that was breathtaking, that even suicides may have known happiness. I sipped, nervous now, at my wine and heard the Andante flow away without fuss, and numbers licked up on the CD player. He murmured from the distance of the carpet and when I caught his eyes he nodded.

'Sibelius.'

'No. Sid Vicious.'

'It had to be one of them, hadn't it.'

Oh, had I wanted to get to know him I could have done so, perhaps, and what wonders might have been revealed. But we were not here for that. And the intellectual jousting was losing its ardour. He sipped at his wine and the glass had become the globe of all the unexplored world in his fingers. Without raising his head he said simply 'Handel,' like a password. I did not ask whether he chose Handel merely to please me. I packed off Sibelius and his Scandinavian chill and suddenly we were listening to the lambent Largo cavatina from Handel's Xerxes. I knew the effect this music had upon me; to me it was a form in music of prayer, nothing less, to listen to the Largo. Ombra mai fù. Handel's last attempt to introduce Italian opera to a raffish London; he might as well have tried to bring it to a town like this one. London clamoured vulgarly for oratorios.

The organ notes lumbered up their scales, and he

shifted his legs and splashed a little white bleed of wine onto the carpet. He looked at the stain settling down into the pile like a boisterous audience at a concert; the strings vibrated slowly, with a great ache of the heart, out of the dwindled notes of the organ introduction. The effect, I thought, was always so ineffably beautiful that the Hindu concept of samadhi came to mind. I felt it was possible to achieve, through listening to the Largo, a gentle communion with an infinite beauty which itself was wisdom; as if a great love had declared itself and waited, waited, for a response. The only possible response was to praise with one's ears. The music flowered, died away, vibrated again and hung on a last sweet chord whose pain lingered in the room like a pietà comprised only of notes until the final cadence relieved it and the organ returned to the theme.

'Haven't you got it sung?'

'No I haven't, sadly. Just the orchestral version.'

My eyes closed in rage and disappointment and the wine and music and his nearness swept over me in a wrap of indignation. Had I got it sung! Who he hell was he to ask me if I had it sung! Well he knew his music, or seemed to. The Largo grew stronger, the presence of intolerable anguish more pronounced. But it all came crashing down around me and I could not rebuild it. Suddenly the music conjured up all the useless intimacies of his life and mine with more to come, and

225

there was only a need to weep, to mourn the spasms of days and months endured turning on the hot spit of some little bastard's careless deceit. Names and faces roared into my mind like dreams as the Largo climbed to its final agony, and I looked down and saw that the young man had closed his eyes and the wine glass sat still, empty, in his long fingers. I could have taken it so easily and smashed it into his face. In my mind's unblinking eye, dead loves rose to mimic and taunt. The music of Handel was gone. It was too painful. I should not adore it so. It opened sad doors. It invited cruelty. One risked one's dignity. I rose quickly as the music concluded and at once, as if a spell had been broken, he raised himself up smartly from his squatting, lolling posture. He had crushed onto his earlier face another one, a mask that resembled a smile, he held forth his glass and in the street a firework crackled. A unicorn, horn spiralling upwards to immortality, bore a dreamer past my darkening window and the air was glazed with a mellow unreality. I knew it was possible to fly above the town, to look down upon the fervour and the dance and praise some earthly goddess for her kindness and feel truly proud of one's paganism. The town had retreated into its egg of stone. Without bothering to look, I imagined stone gorgons had taken on blood and flesh and fluttered upwards with leathery strokes against the damp polished moon, imitating the squeaks of bats.

'More wine, please?'

Handel had entranced him. At least for a moment or two. More fireworks, then, in the street, the wine tasted of vinegar. I stared into the glass as if I expected to see a strange fish swimming there.

'Is your wine alright?'

'It is indeed,' he said. 'Thank you.'

He saluted me with his glass. The fireworks fizzled like champagne. I was surprised to find myself enjoying becoming rather tipsy. I'd forgotten unicorns and strange things that flew past one's window on nights like these. The room wore a sudden cosiness I hadn't noticed a minute before. It felt good to be here. I felt like talking, but I didn't quite know where to begin. The young man crossed and uncrossed his long legs and looked thoroughly at home. We had entered that peculiar place where friendliness has no form, is vague but present like smoke in the room and one is open to its absurdity and simply breathes it in. Cynicism was a component of our game. It drove casual, opening conversation. But as I looked at him now, I felt curiously immune to him.

'I knew a woman once who nursed her dying husband for three years. By the time he died, she thoroughly hated him. Can you imagine that? Love turned into hatred through illness. A topic for research, I would say. She blamed him for robbing her vitality.'

He shuffled his feet. He sipped his wine as if it burned his lips.

'She was an idiot, whoever she was. Someone you knew?'

'No.'

'Liar. Your mother.'

'It's just a story.'

'Why tell it if it's just a story. We all have stories.'

'True to her marriage vows,' I said, remembering her, hearing her sobbing again in the history of myself. 'An Irish Catholic wife. When he died she had a nervous breakdown. His pain had been her salvation. That's almost theological. Through pain, one is saved. Rubbish, of course.'

'Worse than rubbish,' he sniggered. 'It's bollocks. If you want to slip into something more melancholic, I'm off.'

Echoing halls polished to an obscene reflecting texture, her snoring, medicated, beneath a huge and ridiculous crucifix; a building so old Florence Nightingale might have felt at home there, old men pissing themselves and faeces on the toilet floors. The feeling that people had been put out of the way of the world, so that families would be spared their old age and their embarrassing habits. She had died there, surrounded by brilliant white light that fell from a drizzly sky in mid-winter. Her passing seemed to annoy the nurses, who had to clean her up, return her to respectability, make her ready to receive visitors, as it were. In the coffin in the cold and cramped hospital mortuary, her eyelids had not been properly closed. She stared up at me from blank blue eyes. She had been eaten from somewhere deep inside her, and his death had freed her to die.

'You're a Catholic?'

'Once,' I said. 'Not any more.'

'That would account for it. I'm not and never was. Why the fuck are we discussing religion?'

I wanted to get very drunk. It was a sudden decision. Now I didn't care for love-making or anything else. I thought back to that hospital, it's dread rural grey stone misery, Mass bells and benedictions laden with incense and chesty coughs performed somewhere in the distance while I watched her fade away, her hand growing smaller, bonier, less human. There were no omens, no birds crashing against the ancient glass of the single long window. She simply left the room, taking all my belief with her. I'd gradually stopped blessing myself outside churches.

The room had become a sort of tabernacle, and we sat in its drunken holiness passing judgments on this and that, solving the problems of the world, being serious and light by turns. Outside in the streets, the festival grew louder, more insistent, full of blood and laughter; Gaelic blood leaping and churning at the thought of some obscure sacrifice. When, a hundred thousand years after my mother had been deposited in wet Midlands clay, they had found me in the dormitory with my arms around the boy whose name I have never been able to remember, when they expelled both of us into the cold of the world, the mystery of the sacrament performed in the dormitory turned black and blue and filthy by their accusations and lack of faith, lack of belief, they lost two souls forever with the closing of a door. Whatever about him, I became a willing servant of another god, and I believe we had committed no sin until they told us we had been punished.

'I think your confession bit is very crafty,' he said. 'Sin today, confess tomorrow, sin like buggery the day after.'

'Maybe that's why we have so much corruption,' I answered. 'Morality never comes into it. It's all practicality, that's what matters. When I was a kid a priest told me once not to keep wanking because it ruins your clothes.'

The room had grown cold. Just beyond the window a peal of laughter like a broken bell banged cracked against the wind and was carried off. I saw in my mind's eye the deep blackness of the bay and the powerful surge of the Atlantic swell, heaving over histories of dead fishing-boats, currachs, and the jagged wings of flightless aircraft, gently rustling bones and greening precious coins in withered leather satchels, torn pockets, decayed bags. Beyond this carnage lay America in its green dreaming. Beyond that again lay the edge of the world and the oceans tumbled into endless night and fabulous beasts rose up out of the ocean to prey on more men and ships. Further still, heaven lay beyond the North Wind. I refilled our glasses from a new bottle. The wine lolled about like something ill at ease.

'You have to be a hypocrite to be a good Catholic,' he said. 'Queer Catholics are doubly damned.'

'It's a humourless religion.'

'Nothing is perfect. You're not much in the humour department yourself anyway. Can't blame everything on the Holy Ghost.'

I put down my glass. I thought back to the party. Fun for everyone else, perhaps, but for me it had been like attending a funeral at which the corpse hadn't yet arrived. I realised with what grateful speed I had rushed from the party to the square. Yet now came a feeling of raw loneliness that no amount of alcohol and faux-profound chit-chat could dilute.

'Come and sit up here beside me,' I said. He stood up.

'How's that, then?'

'Much more comfortable.'

He leaned in.

'No,' I said. 'I hate kissing the taste of old wine.'

'Hark at fucking me! In that case, a cigarette.' He snapped his fingers.

231

I reached behind me and grabbed the cigarettes. I had not one religious picture, not one crucifix or religious object anywhere in the flat. When I turned back to him that profane miracle of his turning back into a street whore had taken place. I handed him the packet, he took out a cigarette, lit it, put back his head so that I could study, if I wished to, his profile. A bony nose. Roman, some would call it. Not handsome in any strict sense.

'And where are you from?' I asked.

He blew smoke languidly into the room, in control, taking his time, working me.

'Somewhere and nowhere. Ireland's asshole. Take your pick of any small town like this one. I was born in all of them. I have clones out there in every one of them waiting to be resuscitated. I can make my accent sound as if it comes from anywhere you wish. I can even do London: 'Yowrigh, moy son?' Trick of the trade. I don't need a place to come from. Nobody does.'

'Perhaps not. But you do make it sound so...clinical.'

'We may both believe for a time that this is something it isn't. But we know the truth. Wahrheit bildet Sie frei. The truth makes you fee. I learned that in school. We had a German teacher who was queer as a three-pound. Fancied me, he did. It used to drive him wild.'

'You're frank.'

'That's a compliment.'

232

I stood up rather briskly. I disliked him now and I couldn't quite understand why. But I couldn't bear to show him the door.

'Frankness in a whore is a rare commodity.'

'We are all rare commodities. Most of the time we're all whores too. And now you're angry. I'll go if you want. No charge. Sorry for breaking the spell.'

The night was too bloody young. Small hours of the morning alone, while the world played, could kill. No, I couldn't let him go. Perhaps all I wanted was his company. The sound of another voice in the well of my bedroom. A friend of mine told me of a girl, a friend, who had come to his bed the night she had broken off her engagement to some young man or other. They never slept together again, never spoke of it. She had explained that she needed it, his closeness, his physical certainty. Nothing else, just that, for that one time only. No complications; they had remained friends. Was such a thing possible? I guessed he must have felt for her in a way that was not exactly devoid of love, or some similar emotion; could it have been simple lust? They had taken each other, then parted. Perhaps they would never feel that honest with another human being ever again. Something stirred in the pit of my stomach. Not quite nervousness.

'I apologise,' I said. 'I certainly do not want you to go. You confuse me. Or something.'

'Unsettle you.'

233

'Yes, unsettle me. I can't explain it.'

Apparently content with my apology, he sat himself back on the settee. More wine. I was drunk or close enough. The wine swung thickly in the glasses like mercury. I offered him, a sort of making-up treat, an expensive Russian cigarette from a wooden box; someone's gift to me, an affectation. His eyes fluttered deliberately and I imagined druids making finger-language to each other above the heads of the uninitiated. I heard the empty crack of a bottle breaking on street outside. Magic from a waxing moon. The room was suddenly full of half-visible watchers, some wearing hideous masks. Somewhere a man was hauled naked to a bloody stone, the singing rose and continued, driving him mad with terror and longing. I no longer drove myself towards being saved or, for that matter, being sacrificed. I didn't want to be flayed alive or have my heart cut out. I believed in nothing.

'I once knew a woman who painted, for money, tiny models of Irish cottages,' I said, breaking the seal of our silence. 'Carmina was her name, a soft name, a sort of anointed name. In the corner of her work-room stood a guitar that always had five strings, she never bothered to get a sixth. Fifty inch-high models of painted and unpainted thatched cottages.'

On a wall, she had hung a black-and-white print of uncertain provenance depicting a knight holding his sword upwards before him as he knelt through a vigil at

234

the foot of an altar. I wanted often to explain the picture to her, but she showed no sign of wanting it explained. She had slightly oriental eyes. She carried around with her a great weight of sex and it hung in that room like the scent of dying. Later she said, 'I've never been done by a queer before.' And so on and so forth. The tiny houses waited patiently for paint or packaging. I can still see her, relieved of the mystery, discovering that a cock is a cock no matter whose on the end of it, her head flung back messily on her pillow as if she fallen in dirty snow. Now I'm talking about her.

'Can you imagine anything more soul destroying than sitting in a room all day painting little houses,' he says.

There is no point in telling him anything else, he clearly hears what he wants to hear. I ask him to put his arm around my shoulders, an act of solicitude. He's a million miles away, moves like something on strings and is drunk too. His arm feels like the rough crosspiece of a crucifix. I am suddenly nailed to it.

'You think I'm a proper bastard,' he said. His breath, close on me, smelling of iron.

'Not at all.'

There's a huskiness in my voice, as if I had slipped into a trance.

'I don't blame you. Trouble is I'm not a great listener. And I'm not, you know, very affectionate. The way people want you to be. I'm told I should take up meditation, some form of it, anyway.'

I wonder, absurdly, who has told him this, and am amazed that I am a jealous animal, not a very tame one at all, but driven by immediate responses. Is there some other in whom he confides his secret miseries and joys? Are there people who pay him to talk about himself? Any newspaper in the country would offer him a fat cheque to talk about one day of his life. The personal has been taken from us; or did we give it away, like all good whores?

'Have you read the Tao?'

'I've dipped into it,' he said, making an obscene gesture with an index finger, adding, 'Naughty boy. Stand at the back of the class. See me after school.'

'How much difference is there between Yea and Nay?'

'As I say, I've dipped into it. Don't quote things at me.'

'I used to live with a man who taught martial arts,' I lied. Lying, truth-telling: none of that nonsense mattered here. 'He had a beautiful body, glistening. He used to oil it. We'd talk for hours. He'd listen. He'd....'

'Should've held on to him, then. Or was he so busy glistening while he was listening he slipped through your fingers?'

Another obscene gesture. His kiss, when it came, was a tentative child's thing, just about brushing my lips and nothing more. He looked at me and I looked back at him, eye to eye, as lovers and wrestlers do. We drifted off for a while in a comfort of silence. The wine did its work, I thought again about Carmina, the miniature cottages, the fantasy of a martial arts lover covered in oil. The screech of the streets, an animal thing, a fluster, a screen of sound, rose up to us. How often I had wondered how life might possibly be breathed into the waxy dolls skulking at café tables, behind cold windows, entombed in little shrines of indifference? How often had I seen a potential Christ or a Buddha in the freezing gaze of a balding barman, when he poured a glass of blood-red wine or smiled with slitted eyes and no other muscles of his face moving, as if his facial skin were motored from within by tiny selective fleshy wires and wheels? Everything came back to me, folded inside me, and my pain was intense. Perhaps what I really wanted was a Christ or some prophet or holy fool to soothe me, to drift in from the wilderness wild-eyed and starving and lay a hand upon my shoulder and save my soul. No one comes. No miracles follow the stranger down the street. We remain driven by adrenaline, the world's most dangerous drug.

We sat together, his arm still around my shoulders, our glasses glinting like fat candles; and outside the gaiety and flamboyance of the festival tore at the dead silences of the bay and the stony indifference of the little ancient town. Then he said:

237

'My arm's gone dead.'

And he promptly removed it from around my
shoulders. Where his arm had rested, a dark chill
descended. The odour of Russian tobacco was
everywhere on him. Another slop of wine dropped a
thousand feet to the carpet. The room would stink
come morning. He sat upright, as if recovering his
dignity, regretting everything. On cue, I stood up and
scrabbled, on the edge of tears, for a CD of Bach's
Brandenburg Concertos; the Minueto contained
poltergeist noises, presumably recorded on the original
tape through some technical fault or other, unpleasant
sounds as if someone were trying to vomit, coda'd
with a whispering whistle before the oboes fell in. The
sounds disturbed me and I turned the music off.
Somewhere in the black mouth of the bay a foghorn
sounded as if in protest. I imagined fogs, thick and
prodigious as milky cancers, edging over the waters,
swallowing whole chunks of sea; at last, swallowing
the moon like an aspirin.

He went to the window and looked down. The
streets were blazing now, you could feel their heat;
bagpipes, shouting, abrupt sexual laughter, fireworks,
the occasional melancholy roll of song. What emotions
the spectacle stirred in him I could only guess.
Perhaps, for all I knew, he looked upon life itself as a
show to be ended with the rustle of a curtain. He
would stay and the cold gnaw of the night would heal.

I stood up, placed my hands on his hips. He did not move. I saw what he saw, a scattering of gaudy young people in steepled hats, many-coloured kerchiefs and jaunty hose. Above all of this a foghorn bleated and a guitar strummed; it might have well been a lute. Did a unicorn prance out of a thicket somewhere under the admiring moon, mysteries coming and going in the flashes of smiles, the thrumming music, the stinging wine? The town seemed to have somersaulted, thrown itself backwards, tumbled over upon itself and been reborn into the age it celebrated, eight-hundred years younger, religion, fantasy and lust understood as a weaving of the same cloth, curious adventurers gathering to throw themselves and their shops over the edge of the world into the maw of Hell. I saw my face, and I saw his, acknowledged the iconographic we established in the window. If anyone looked up and saw us, how might be be interpreted? I squeezed his hips gently. He murmured, a ghost of a sound. I placed a kiss quivering and indistinct upon the edge of the collar of his shirt. I drank in the thick odour of his hair. Voluptas – the Latin had it, the joy one takes in pleasure. No word in English quite conveys it and fills the mouth like tender grapes about to spill their wine as that word, voluptas.

But, to spoil it all, there came into my thoughts unbidden a long cement grey promenade beside an indifferent sea, and the figure of a small girl pushing a wheelchair in which sits a young man whose head is shorn of hair, sickly, pouting as the wind spray spits up from the black rocks; her eyes squint, she dislikes having to push him and all love has gone out of it. She trundles him into the damp wind as if hoping the salt will dissolve them both and for a moment her nose runs until she flicks up a hand to clear it. He hair is raggled by wind and responsibility, the way a wine-drinker flounders into a state of uncaring: it starts with the hair. She carries nothing for herself because he has sucked away the reason for love in becoming ill and dependent.

I stood behind my young man, for he was mine now and I knew it; and I saw again the figure of this young girl, an icon in itself, describing more agony endured in silence than most people ever encounter. I had wanted to grab the invalid from her dutiful fingers and fling him into the guffawing sea.

Suddenly disturbed, I turned away from him and away from the window. He looked after me. I was close to tears and it was all absurd. I sat down on the settee and gave myself a Russian cigarette. Nervous. He moved across to me and I noticed the frown crease his features.

'Oh, well. In these times, it's nice to see people enjoying themselves.'

A dab of peevishness.

'Good for them,' I said. I pulled hard on my cigarette.

240

'Don't let their good humour kill your sparkling mood, or anything.'

I wondered again where he came from and whether his education had worked against him; in a land whose memory is still a mulch of rural evictions, deceits, small deals done behind pub doors, any scrap of learning marks a person as the enemy of the common good. The rural world we inhabited: how bitter and envious it was, even as failed tycoons hanged themselves in their garages, even as others built houses on flood-plains. The newspapers churned the offal of our slaughtered dignity into the angers and self-hatreds we lived on day to day; we talked of nothing else, we lived for the failure of others. How had he survived? How could love of any sort survive in a mire of self-delusion? Had we not all become whores? He had perhaps grown up in a household where white-thorn bushes were as sacred, or he'd run his adolescence through the sieve of one of those small town housing estates where nothing happens and the ice-cream van tours every evening at the same time. A single shop half a mile away. In any case, like most of us, he'd lost sight of the New Jerusalem.

I remembered a newspaper that had carried a story about a failed bank on one page and, on another, the discovery of the remnants of a Black Mass in a village graveyard. We had not moved forward eight hundred years, we had dragged those years behind us, a shadow that no light could disperse. It was quite possible that the laughing festival in the street did not exist at all. I too believed in the godlings of river and grove; like Skelton, I obeyed the priest in me and paid homage to the poet. I was the swinging tycoon tied to a garage roof-beam while skimpy light flashed on the bonnet of the expensive car I could no longer afford; I was the priest hiding under the skirts of his bishop; the disgraced politician ennobled for his disgrace in the one-street hamlet where he was king.

'You are religious,' I said. 'I bet you are. Underneath it all.'

'Where did that come from? The only thing I have underneath it all, Mr Joyful, is my rod and my staff.'

'I once wanted to be a priest.'

'I think all Catholic queers do. They're in love with the figure on the crucifix, that delicious squirming agony in a loincloth. It's their first encounter, kneeling on a hard step, adoringly staring through incense, just before they walk their first boy to some shady nook to inspect his cranny, hypnotised by his transparent skin and his flaw - less blue eyes and the way his calves move in his scruffy short trousers. You don't have to explain to me, brother.'

I held out my hand and touched his cheek with my fingers.

'I don't know where all this is coming from. All that noise in the back room. It's like we're on the set of a play.'

'We are. We always have an audience, even if it just comprises ourselves.'

'I am a whore,' I said. He kissed me on the forehead, I bowed my head slightly to accept it. 'I will do anything you want.'

'Less of the Garbo melodrama.'

He kissed me again, three, four kisses light as air on my forehead. I had an erection but I had tears gathering in the corners of my eyes. I could smell ancient floor polish and see the dormitory door opening, the boy under me whimpering but even then I wouldn't stop.

'Sit down on the floor.'

I could not do otherwise. He wiped a slick tear from my eye. The foghorn, sitting on its rat-choked island in the middle of the bay, moaned like a fat man making love. This time he made the move, resting his scented head upon my shoulder. I caressed his hair, odours of grass and salt. I asked him whether he wanted more wine.

'I'm sleepy,' he said. 'Doped me, have you?'

'You should have said you had a headache.' I spoke softly, as if he were a very small child.

He closed his eyes.

'You have a nice gaff here,' he said, 'And you seem like a good Catholic boy.'

'Tell me about yourself.'

'We've been through that. I don't get paid for

243

giving interviews. Well, there wouldn't be enough money in the world for my story. Or you wouldn't have it, anyway.'

'That terrible?' I was whispering now.

'That ridiculous.'

I wanted to keep his head just where it was forever and not continue our dance to its ultimate pas de deux. He opened his eyes then and looked up at me, and his eyes mirrored reflected everything the light held in the room. I stood up, took his hand. He snatched up a Russian cigarette. Nothing was rushed. At the door of the bedroom, it was he who switched on the light. My bedroom embarrassed me even though I worked hard to keep it scrupulously tidy. Posters from French galleries, a framed photograph of myself as a small boy, taken by God knows whom. A light beige quilt. He turned to me – now he, apparently, had me by the hand. I was hesitating and he could feel it. A cautious application of brakes on a gently sloping hill.

'It's hardly your first time,' he said. 'It's like riding a bicycle.'

I couldn't explain. The essence of all of this should have been simplicity. Complications became murderous and restricting. I saw myself handing him money in the morning, bruised by the lovelessness of it all, trying to re-imagine the sex by way of consolation. I turned off the sitting-room light and a

244

rocket burst beyond our window, showering the dark room with a blink of yellow light. He ran his hands over the quilt. He admired a small reproduction of a National Gallery painting by Orpen. I remembered it, a gift from a stout but polite man who had given me lunch, and later pretended to be nervous. A man who grunted. He saw the telephone.

'Goody! Room service!'

The remark broke the tension. He sat down on the bed and took off his shoes.

Revived, I jumped up.

'At your command!'

'Wine! Wine! Wine!' he said, in a sort of mock bleating.

I went into the sitting-room, putting on the lights again, then grabbing the bottle and scuttling back, already his servant, much as I had told him I could be. It was a new bottle and I had had to work the thick suck of the fridge door. The wine was chilled and ached in my hand. When I got back to my bedroom he was under the quilt, his hands happily joined behind his head. He'd piled his clothes on the floor – did he not like to undress in front of me? Little tufts of hair braided his breast and nipples as if he had just glued them on for effect.

'Now this is the way,' he said; 'In style and comfort. Can I call you Jeeves?'

'Fuck off. No.'

All that remained was to penetrate the silence that brooded over the room like the finishing note of a symphony. I must have smiled – don't lovers always smile, at such a moment? – and I entered my own room as if I were a stranger, bearing gifts. Sounds up from the street, the gearwheels of a small town grinding. I was overcome with shyness. He saw it.

'I would never have taken you for shy.' He'd changed the tone of his voice again; this time he sounded like a no-nonsense matron in a dingy hospital. I resented this, of course. I wished he'd shut up and just be nobody at all. Instead, I replied to him.

'It's odd,' I said, wanting to slap him. 'Maybe we've talked too much.'

'Best not to talk with your mouth full. Condom!'

He was helpless beneath the quilt. I started dashing about the bedroom, found the condoms.

'A bit of foreplay first, no?'

How could he have resisted if I had thrown myself at him, claws bared? At the same time, I was oddly moved by his vulnerability.

'The talk was the foreplay.'

'Maybe if I turn out the light,' I said, like a blushing bride.

'Well, do, but don't drop the wine, and unless you've night-vision how are you going to put that damned thing on properly?'

Farce, of course. Humiliation. I saw his eyes

246

gleaming with silly confidence; they seemed to gleam more brightly in the dark. He had all the time in the world. I undressed, tottering, at the foot of the bed while he stared at me as if I wasn't there, as if he'd seen too many men undress and was immune to it all.

I raised the quilt, the single sheet, felt it flutter up a breeze that carried his musk into my nostrils full of dark spices and the clean sweat of cold nights. I imagined I was his first that evening. He smelled of himself, a cocktail of hardness and surgical tenderness, exquisitely exciting. My bedclothes tasted of launderettes. I slid beneath them like a knife into its sheath. He turned in the dark and the lithe rope of his arm moved over the taut pit of my belly. I groped backwards and my fingers clutched the sweaty neck of the wine bottle. He had become eager, there was something vulgar about it. He wanted to do the business, if you like. I was unprepared. I fumbled with the condom, he helped me. Humiliating. Now that we were lying together in bed, our bodies gradually dissolving into a sort of familiarity, I needed ritual. I sat up on the darkness and raised the bottle. He sighed. Was he bored? Had I treated him too carefully? I thought of the dead idea of some good music, good wine and decent conversation and felt I had made a fool of myself. A weight shifted in my chest and I felt terribly alone. I poured two drinks in the dark, handed him one, feeling some cold wine dribble over my fingers. Anonymous territories; winter descendant. He sipped and I felt him watch me with his animal night-vision; he pulled himself upright, releasing his fragrances of flesh and desire. Yet again from the streets, a gout of laughter, a crackle of glass. Dieser Liebe toller Fasching: Heine took opium for his pain. Gautier, Dumas, on watch by his bed, along with Sand, who seven years later watched Chopin die. So much for the great carnivals of love; it all came down to meat against meat, the poets were deceived. Or deceived themselves. It mattered little which.

My abstractions turned melancholy, I blamed too much wine and as a consequence I drank in gulps. My mood had become a wall against which he could make no headway. The bedside lamp tossed crazy mountain shapes against the ceiling. One shift of a knee brought whole continental ranges tumbling. The neurasthenic smoke of the Russian cigarettes circled, melted, circled again. I moped to myself that it wasn't fair, I'd brought him back for gaiety and I had managed to encircle myself with a ring of what amounted to mourning. For what?

He was not responsible, certainly. Neither, in some way, was I. A mood had altered in the very air itself. A fluctuation of the influences of the moon? All sex, I know, is preceded by a weighty and mostly mock gravitas not unlike that through which wills are read out. I have never found it, for example, humorous, as some have; which is why I cried out, an effort to fulfil myself, as it were, to mark myself as being present at all. A stab through the heart. The wine level dropped in the bottle and his agile fingers crawled over my penis in a tragic effort to arouse me. Little happened. More than anything I felt the need to talk, the subject was irrelevant; drowsiness filtered my imagination. I ran my fingers through his dark hair absentmindedly, as if he were a small dog.

For no reason I can determine I was reminded of nights spent in dilapidated snooker-halls, warrens of loneliness, each table draped in a shroud of light. My lover from the knick-knack shop – and how was he getting along at this moment? – whispering to me, in words borrowed from some late-night radio DJ, 'I suppose I could find something stimulating about the working classes. Excellent ball-control. Lots of practice.' The coloured balls clacked like the beads of an abacus. Each ball contained its pellet of frozen golden light as it ran across the green baize pursued by the suggestive lunge of the tipped cue. The green table was as soft under the fingertips as the rim of a hat from Jermyn Street. Faces made old by concentration and worklessness hung like ceremonial masks in the tents of light. The silence was clinical, expectant, reverential. Anything louder than a whisper was vulgar and heads looked up. There was something sacral about the graceful waltzing around the green altars. Time oozed out between the shining running balls, brass indicators scrapped along the rails of scoreboards, there was the faint odour of chalk and whole unmoving clouds of cigarette smoke. I could not play very well and it took me some time of embarrassed watching to find an idle player. Glad to be taken on, I played with the tactless hunger of a child and laughed away my errors. Players at other tables thought my guffaws insulting to the game and stared at me. My partner won, of course, but without satisfaction, and this showed in his face. Off-table conversation concerned work on the docks, closures, the who's who of a dole office. I wondered what sort of pleasures were available to these men. For in truth no one here seemed to be enjoying their game, it was all too serious and anxious. The snooker hall was sanctuary. Two players followed me into the lavatory and cursorily beat me about the shoulders with cues and bruised my arms and drew a cut over my right eye. I slunk in tears from the hall that night, and never returned. My falderol shop-owner harrumphed like a small walrus.

'Ah, the rougher edge of the handshake! Such people do not think, in any real sense of the word. They react. They have been doing so all their lives. They live on a primal level – naïve of you to imagine any thing else. They can smell your difference, prowling the outside of their cave. Poverty has no imagination. Poor you.'

250

I plucked at the strands of hair on the head of this idle young man from the streets, or wherever he came from, and felt the hurt of that past rejection. To where, and to whom, did I belong? If not snooker-halls and queer parties, if not the guttural language of lavatories, then where?

It was in this very bed that, more than once when he was too drunk to find his way home, my shop-owner friend and I had made love, or tried to, and the memory came back, naturally. I had known some loving from that otherwise careless man. The pain came, consequently, in spurts. Then another remembrance: an unmarried friend of mine who took two women lovers, very different in temperament, explaining:

'I have sides to my personality. One is delicate, ornamental, a closet of frilly underwear. The other has an accent like a rusty saw and is a street-sweeping mugger by trade. So by my women. When I go down on the first I taste talc and oysters and she turns her head, closes her eyes, and all of that false shame. With the second, I taste rainy street-gutters, gussets losing their elastic, the sweat of a day standing on her feet behind the counter of a store where she is constantly demeaned. But when she comes there is no false modesty, she thrashes with her murderous hips, hinting at some deep private violence. Now to lose one of these women and be forced to keep up with the other would be true loneliness, as if I had been sawn in half. All true love comes from loneliness.'

He envied men who could be happy with one woman. He married in the end, had children, is relatively happy. He is not, like so many, to be found in Saturday nightclubs with his wedding ring in the back pocket of his ill-fitting expensive jeans. Which woman did he marry? Neither, of course. He married a third, the one who had remained invisible until the last minute, the one about whom he never said a word.

When love forfeits its emotion, the dry bed of what is left is strewn with terrors and vague anxieties, that scuttle – if they move at all – across the abandoned heart. In the middle of the night one wakes up sweating, afraid of the dark. We worry about the penis that gave us such pleasure and might also kill us. 'I am not afraid of you,' I shouted at him, the first time he slapped my face with his open hand. But I was always afraid, if not of him, then of his cock or the world.

Once he said he'd take me to Paris. O luminous city! O Piaf dreams and men who knew how to dress! The clubs! But he didn't take me. He sent me back vividly-coloured postcards of the Eiffel Tower and the Moulin Rouge as if I were an ignorant country-boy who collected postcards of strange places and pinned them on my wall. Each one was like an X-ray of his heart; this is what he thought of me, this and this only. He nonetheless brought me back a salmon pink pullover from the Galeries Lafayette on the boulevard

252

Haussmann; perhaps so that when I finally, months later, discovered the photo of himself smiling with his arm round a thin African outside the nearby Opéra Garnier, I wouldn't feel so bad. The price-tag wouldn't come off the pullover and in trying to cut it away I snagged part of the sleeve, as if the pullover was destined to be marked as a failure. What in God's name was he doing with me all that time? O luminous city!

A wind smacked off the bay over the roofs and skittered against the window. I poured the last of the wine. He takes the drink but has questions in his eyes.

'We'll be too tired, soon.'

'We're too fucking tired now. The moment has passed, as they say.'

'Yes.'

In that single word it's as if I have cancelled the night. He turned away, a soft slide of his rough thigh against mine in the dark. Then his free hand crept over my limp cock. It stirred, still dull and unwilling, a drunk disturbed in his dozing. A phrase came into my head unbidden:

'Sulphuric acid is the only suitable acid because nitric acid itself is an oxydising agent, and hydrochloric acid does not afford any free oxygen.'

At fifteen I had no use for such information and had eyes and intellect only for my History teacher, a flimsy man in spectacles. And when I walked to bus-stops with my short-trousered fellow secondary schoolboy, was that the real beginning? Or was there any beginning at all? True questions are too weighty for notebooks. But I began a diary full of lies and distortions, full of what I left out. How could I write that when the History teacher adjusted his spectacles and spoke passionately about Sir Thomas Wentworth, Lord Deputy – curbing the power of the Irish gentry and forcing them to restore Church lands which they'd absorbed into their own peevish estates – my teenage heart faltered and my hands were damp? New rain pummelled the window. Beside me, my young bed-mate sighed dramatically.

As if summoned up by the brightening wind, a knock at the door. My young man's hand emerged from beneath the sheets like a fish darting from beneath a rock. A tremor of apprehension. Nothing much to say. We still fear discovery, even now. I shout a throaty 'Yes!' and the knocking comes again. I pull on my trousers and sweep a shirt about my shoulders and close over the bedroom door.

I opened my door on the face of a faun, complete with roseate snout. A white frilled neckpiece, a dark cloak about the thin shoulders. Behind this figure, in a shadow, its familiar; a tiny young woman in another tapering tall hat and floor-length furling dress, a tight colourful bodice and a scanty veil drawn about her mouth and nose. A moth leaped in the trapped light of the stairway. A door slammed in the burly wind. A dog barked. A drunken voice laughed. The girl clears her throat and the faun speaks, forcing up some authority behind the mask.

'Is this Twenty-One. Is this where the party is?'

'No. This is Eighteen.'

'Fuck off or fuck us!' came a loud voice from my bedroom.

Through the mask he inspected the gilt numerals nailed to my door. Perhaps I was lying. Somewhere overhead, as if to confirm what I've said, a woman laughed and the rhythmic sexual thud of some heavy metal banged out.

'Upstairs,' said the veiled girl. 'Come on!'

'Sorry,' said the faun. 'I think we've found it.'

He bowed histrionically, the girl giggled. My heart slowed. They turned upstairs. I closed the door. Their youth and exuberance had winded me. I needed masks and veils more than they. My shop-owner ex-lovers were in my head like the mantras of a catechism: You always pay. We don't get away with it. Sod the change in attitudes. Those who suffer most pay in instalments. Life on the never-never.

I can hear the girl's voice as they go upstairs. God help us, but they started to argue.

'You said you wanted to bring me,' the girl said. 'But you'd've brought that other cunt if you had the chance. Take your paw off my arse!'

I could not catch his reply. Perhaps he knew the uselessness of making one. Nothing is perfect, disguises or no disguises. I pity her. Perhaps she will cry tonight, or in the light of morning. A waste.

My young man, clearly out of utter boredom, had fallen asleep, wrapped like something unborn in a fat membrane of bedclothes. So I wasn't able to chastise him for his rude remarks. I had a cigarette, sitting in the dark on the edge of the bed, careful not to wake him. I heard the dampened thudda-thudda from upstairs and I wondered about a sleeping pill. Rather, a whole bottle of them, down on top of the wine, over and out. A churchbell tonged out over the town. Rain animated the light I speckles and slicks like oil on the window and I imagined the tattered liquefying pictures of the world outside without looking for them. Waves of fatigue crashed over me like smoke from a hot fire. I stubbed out the cigarette in a dead cluttered ashtray. For the first time in a long time I slumped to my knees at the foot of the crumpled bed and joined my hands and muttered 'Our Father, which art....'

But, of course, I was merely praying to the figure in the bed.

\*　　\*　　\*

The great Egg of the World had split asunder, spilling a gently warming yolk of liquid sunlight over the carpeted floor of the bedroom and over the hill-country of the bed.

256

Reborn, remade, the room murmured with the odours of stale wine and cigarettes, the lost incense of all rooms of love. Or, in my case, of no love. Poets, with their easy and ridiculous licence, have endowed the clumsy real world with a lie of rose petals and musk, of sated torpor without the lambent embarrassment. Nonetheless, when my eyes broke upon the drowsing room, I was surprised to find myself at some sort of peace. I had slept in spite of myself. Perhaps my prayers had redeemed me.

He lay still sleeping, one arm crooked backwards around his head, defenceless, innocent, in a wreck of bedclothes. He was untouched, at least by me. I slipped out of bed, tucked him in, kissed one of his creamy shoulders and padded like a murderer into the kitchen. After a time the smells of coffee percolating and eggs frying alerted the small animal in him. He coughed, shuffled into the kitchen like a girl, with small feeble steps. Almost because we had not made love or perpetrated any act resembling it, there was something weirdly precious and warm about his presence. Recalling the run of the evening's events as if it were a timetable at no point along which we had boarded a train, I tossed the eggs and listened, strangely content, to the nervous bubbling of the coffee. I opened a window, the glare stung my eyes. The street below was devastated, horribly lonely, papers fluttered like dead birds in a damp yellow wind, coloured ribbons and pennants flicked around each other in accidental caresses. I was dressed by the time I carried to the table a tray of eggs, toast, milk, sugar, butter, mugfuls of hot coffee. He watched me, not uttering a word. He ate as if hunger were no stranger to him, that is, he ate without the least self-consciousness.

Lines from Henri Michaux, mescaline addict, poet, sailor, rambled over to me and whispered themselves into my sleepy ears:

> He who is here is no longer clad
> he is out of the body and the desert feeds him...

Like the head of an unruly Venetian prince from some drapery or other stuffed in a book, his damp-sleeped head hovered over the pale nimbus of his plate. By such iconography were the gods made flesh. In the street, the dreary timpan of motorbikes, the grating of gears. The town is rising from sleep, ashamed of its first nakedness. I did things around the rooms, tidied this, put away that. A cough, a clot of sound, upstairs; someone is struggling to find a radio station. I imagine a faun's mask under a chair, discarded and soon to be part of the rubbish of another day.

I have put on something slow by Mozart by the time he staggers into the sitting-room. The strings hum in the early light and motes of dust wander about in the air like drunken party-goers. He feels his chin. Partly, I think, because that's what's normal to do in the mornings. Our play has not reached its final act.

'I feel so rough.'

I hand him a cigarette.

'Too early for me. You wouldn't have a razor, would you? Disposable, of course.'

'I do indeed. A packet in the bathroom. On the shelf.'

'Great stuff. You're a star.'

He shuffled off and as he leans his head to one side I saw, like an indecipherable tattoo on the arm of a sailor, a tiny point of perforation on the lobe of his ear. I hadn't noticed a ring in his ear all evening. Perhaps he once wore it in memory of something that no longer existed. The pull of this petty secret was suddenly irresistible. I want explanations. The coffee is tugging at my brain. I feel powerless. The room brightened up with the Eb Concertante, and outside the windows Hitchcockian birds squealed and ranted. He went into the bathroom and closed the door over with a faint huffing sound.

I scribbled a cheque. He hadn't asked for money, but there's a weird etiquette amongst some of them, where asking is vulgar and embarrassing. I had already relegated him to some other order; he is them. I had moved away from him, and made the gesture physical by moving across the sitting-room to the window; the street was crushed, out of breath, the early mornings of every small town. As if bathed in a nocturnal sweat, the street has a floss, a sheen. Beyond the marquee's quivering poles the bay silvered and shivered like a mirror made of mercury. I forced open the window against generations of dust and grime. The routine excitements of the streets rushed in to reassure me, shrouds of scattering vehicle engines, pattering feet, shouts like tears in the morning's fabric. I closed my eyes and allowed the cold air to brush against my eyelids and my heart fluttered gently, as if the salty air had turned the fragile sails of my soul. I felt renewed, awake. I wanted him out of the flat.

The effect was liberating but in a crazy way. I saw him approaching from the bathroom and waved the cheque at him. The cheque desanctified everything, every word we had spoken between us, every move we'd made; it erased every note of tenderness, every breath of understanding. Everything began to turn to dust and at the same time I seemed to grow stronger, more determined. He looked at me, glanced at the cheque. He was drying his hair in a blue towel.

'Did you sleep?'

'Very well, thanks,' he replied. 'And you?'

'Take it. We were both drunk. That's the way it is.'

'That's the way it is,' he said, shrugging his shoulders. He put the towel aside, ran his fingers through his hair. 'I'll get dressed now and leave you alone.'

He flung himself out of the room. That's the way it is. Your own misery turns into a queer sort of strength which isn't quite self-loathing; you assuage all of that with the cheque. He's goods you've purchased. Your loneliness won't set in again for some hours. He's been a drug, of sorts, and he won't wear off for a time. Then you'll drag the street again, or some pub. I could always visit my shop-owner and beg to be taken back, humiliate myself, cause a scene, threaten to cut my wrists. The stage would be set for that; he, early-morning-wrapped in some other man's legs, a dishevelled bedroom, me in hysterics waving a razor.

I sat down on the settee and had a cigarette. Forget the Russian ones now, this was real life. Any cigarette will do once the stage-crew have moved in to clear the theatre. I let him get dressed undisturbed. He was wearing his jacket when he came into the room.

'Look,' he said. He moved towards me with a hand outstretched.

'Yes?'

'Nothing happened last night?'

'No. It didn't. We didn't fuck, I was too drunk. '

'Not what we had in mind, then.'

I looked at the tip of my cigarette. Somewhere a star illuminated a universe no bigger than this room.

'I was glad of your company. Money for nothing, if you like. Money for filling an empty space. You've earned this. Business is business.'

261

He looked at the cheque. I thought, Christ, he was going to cry.

Mozart was spiralling to a close. I wanted him to go. The music slowed.

'Mozart,' he said. 'At this hour of the morning. I lied, you know.'

'God knows what about. I don't. This is all about lying. If you don't take the cheque I'll tear it up and toss the bits out the window. Maybe you along with it.'

He had turned annoyingly boyish and fragile. I didn't want someone else's fragility. I had enough of my own. I didn't want some we'll-always-have-Paris bullshit. I'd had enough; of him, of myself, of the new day being born.

But he came over and very quickly placed both his hands on my face and kissed me, drawing me to him, roughly, not a hint of gentleness. I struggled, turned my face away. His wet mouth broke upon my cheeks, my lips like a hot ugly wave. There was, I felt, an insult implied in the kiss.

'Bastard,' he whispered, and allowed me to pull away.

I stood up and slapped him hard. Once, twice. He staggered back against the CD player. There was a trickle of blood at the side of his mouth. He wiped it with his hands and looked at the red smear on his fingers, surprised, indignant. Then he stared at me.

'You put any of that near me and I'll kill you.'

I heard the words rush out of my mouth as if I were a ventriloquist's dummy and someone else, someone brutal and full of hatred, had uttered them. But I didn't regret them. We were watching each other. He looked again and again at the smear of blood on his fingers and then he began to cry, to weep, his face destroyed, ugly, red under the weeping. He tried to straighten himself up. He was weeping great gouts of tears, his mouth sticky now and grotesque and repellent.

'I never took money in my life,' I heard him say. 'I never took money in my fucking life.'

'You put on a damned good show.'

'I thought that was what you wanted. I didn't know what you wanted. I didn't know what I should be for you. Fuck me, man, everybody wants to be something.'

'Get out.'

He closed the door and disappeared. I stood there with the cheque in my hand. The silence when he was gone was chilled and sickly. For a moment I did not know what had happened. Perhaps he was in an adjacent room? No, he was gone. I didn't look out of the window. Bells pealed; the mysteries he carried with him, children's secrets, like mine, were no longer worth knowing. I was alone again and the cold weight pressed prematurely against my heart. Even the street sounds could not penetrate the gathering silence, which seemed peculiar to my being in this room alone.

263

I smoked again and listened. Old ghosts of remote mornings stood in the corners and watched me. What will he do now? they seemed to ask. The world was, once again, flawed. Cut in two. For each night I had purchased to describe an arc about my emptiness there had been the hard coin of mornings of guilt. I consoled myself, as we all do, that no two days could be quite the same.

Big notes rolled like rocks down the wet sides of steeples. Town of holy bells and Crusaders' tombs, of leering gryphons, coloured windows over which marriage-stones of festering families fell into the streets grain by stony grain. The sea conquering all, borne up out of the wind in licks of salt. Words are so much trash.

So for some reason my next cigarette was Russian, and I sat by the window without looking out, imagining it, streets drying under a light breeze peppered with grains of sand and salt needle-sharp. The smoke snaked upwards towards a ceiling creaking under someone's to and fro tread. My room had the acrid stale odour of a cell. When at last the cigarette died in an ashtray I began to see him, tears drying on his face, navigating the his private labyrinth of streets; how far had he managed to get? Already his mystery was dissolving. The decaying marriage-stones, the weary gryphons, will lean over him dumbly as he vanishes among them. Would he remember me? They seldom do. One puts up with that. The faces change, like the conversations, but part of the dark magic is that they remain the one face, the one conversation, held over and over. Was there any point along the shipwreck of our night where we might have become friends, longing to laugh again, sip wine again, at another time? An agreement of intellects? I had laughed long and often with my shop-owner. I had laughed even as the curtains were noisily falling down. He had warned me not to try to assuage loneliness with further loneliness. Oh, the conversation we had had, the effervescent unions of body and soul! How could they be repeated? I wondered how his party had gone and realised that I was standing up now with a fresh bottle of wine in my hand, sucking from the neck. His shop of nick-knacks, tin soldiers, old fiddles, Georgian windows, wood-and-plastic metamorphosis, light effulgent in the tumbler-glass panes like split fire. Is that his drunken ghost climbing the stairs? I throw up in the sink, wash my mouth out with wine, slug it back where it bites the throat and burns the belly. If I thought I could bring that young man back I would wade into the waking Elizabethan streets and summon him back with shouts and clamours.

A bus roared by and faded, engine hammering through a broken exhaust pipe. I was steady and the lump in my throat choked me. I left the room clutching the bottle. We are Cagliostros, all of us, great

265

deceivers, jokers with our hearts sewn on our flamboyant sleeves. Sleeves of flame. Pucker up, our lips welcome graces falling from the ungodly sky like petals from graveyard flowers. I walked in the streets as if I were invisible; people passed through me as I passed through them. Dogs patrolled the gutters. Children skittered their way to school. I straightened my back, but it stooped again, and wine slopped out of the bottle like blood from a wound.

At my shop-owner's door I paused, allowing small noises to penetrate the painted wood. I drank thickly, almost to the point of nausea again. I hummed a tune. I was absolutely in my right mind. Something fluttered like snow past my eyes. I shook my head and knocked.

I believe I thought of nothing at all when he opened the door. He was fully dressed and a little surprised, but not as surprised as I thought he might have been. I would have no more beautiful falsehoods. I saw myself reflected in his eyes. The stranger with whom he'd passed his night fluttered out of the bedroom and into the bathroom, snibbing the door. We had been lovers in the manner of the greatest lovers of the world, with desperation, and temporarily. He looked at me and at the bottle in my hand, and he was not afraid.

The author wishes to acknowledge
and thank *STAND* magazine, for publishing
'At the Reichstag Hotel'.

# In Praise of Fred Johnston's Writing

'In planting his flag in potentially alienating turf, Johnston continues on an Irish literary path closer to Beckett or Joyce than say, Ross O'Carroll Kelly or Cecilia Ahern, and justly *The Neon Rose* will remain a frightening prospect to readers of the latter writers.'
Kiran Acharya – Culture Northern Ireland.org

'But then in these quiet images, and in the "decent[ness]" of 'sex being careful", the poet also subtly and carefully reveals a certain "mad[ness]": a world where abuse and suffering are masked and silenced.'
Review of poetry collection *The Oracle Room* – Ben Wilkinson, in *Eyewear*.

'Shot through with the narrator's feverish, almost Gothic imagination, both Johnston's novel and its eponymous heroine are resonant creations.'
*Transcript Review* of the novel *Atalanta*

'The stories are strong, with an underlying emphasis on music, but the prose has been lyrical and sensitive. There is movement here, a gentle rhythm, and along with this, a real sense of the tragedy and sometimes futility of life.'
Review of short stories, *Keeping The Night Watch* – Des Kenny in Kennys.ie

# PARTHIAN

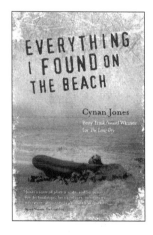

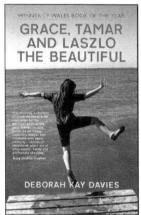

www.parthianbooks.com